Hurricane Party

Steve Brown

Chick Springs Publishing
Taylors, SC

First published in the USA in 2002 by
Chick Springs Publishing
PO Box 1130, Taylors, SC 29687
E-mail: ChickSprgs@aol.com
Web site: www.chicksprings.com

Library of Congress Control Number: 2002141143
Library of Congress Data Available

ISBN: 0-9712521-5-7

10   9   8   7   6   5   4   3

Author's Note

This is a work of fiction. Names, characters, places, and incidents are the product of the author's imagination or are used fictitiously. Any resemblance to actual events, specific locales, organizations, or persons, living or dead, is entirely coincidental and beyond the intent of either the author or the publisher.

Acknowledgments

For their assistance in preparing this story, I would like to thank C.B. Berry, Mark Brown, Missy Johnson, Jackie Kellett, Kate Lehman, Matt McCoy, Ann Patterson, Kimberly Medgyesy, Susan Snowden, and my favorite Gen-Xer, Stacey. And, of course, Mary Ella.

For Agatha Christie

Not everything you learn
has to come from firsthand experience.

—Susan Chase

Chapter 1

It was supposed to be a hurricane party.
It turned out to be an invitation to murder.

Chad has a problem. Me.

I've always been a problem for the boy. Yes, yes, I love my main man, but there's this thing between us, a guy thing that weighed heavily on my mind as I peddled my bike through the rain of the approaching storm. While I'm out chasing down the bad guys, Chad can't be satisfied with merely building some of the most beautiful boats to be found along the Grand Strand.

You can tell your man just so many times how proud you are of his accomplishments, but always in his head is the fact that I'm the one who kicks in doors and brings in the bad guys. I carry a Lady Smith & Wesson—don't leave home without it. Chad carries a briefcase filled with designs of his latest watercraft. You'd think being that creative would be enough, but it's not, and that brings us back to the hurricane party.

It was September and hurricane season had been busy. Charleston had already been threatened, as had Myrtle Beach, and a storm by the name of Josephine was wandering around in the Gulf of Mexico. Nothing had hit us. Yet. But Hurricane Lili was on her way. She was going to smack right into the Grand Strand, and people were headed inland. The smart ones, that is. Evidently, I was engaged to one of the other sort. My fiancé had accepted an invitation to a hurricane party.

Why were we riding bicycles? Well, motorbikes and cars don't run all that well after being submerged in saltwater when a storm has passed through. We had left Chad's Corvette beyond the Intracoastal Waterway, parking close to Little River, and ridden in from there, avoiding any safety patrols trying to protect us from ourselves.

It had been tough sledding. Sometimes the wind was in our faces, sometimes it tried to blow us over. We rode in low gear most of the way, and because of the rain, we wore the appropriate attire, laminated Gore-tex: Chad's a bright blue, mine a dull lifeguard red. Large packs on our backs held in place by frames made us an easy target for gusts up to twenty miles per.

My rain gear was a holdover from the days when I'd been a lifeguard and finder of runaways, before graduating to private investigating and finally to SLED, the investigative arm of the government of South Carolina, officially called the State Law Enforcement Division.

Hurricane Hugo had been my party and once was enough. The sound the wind makes is like a train rumbling through, or whispering to you all night long. And you'd better have your house boarded up because it could end up in the second row. Second row is anything off the beach, and when hurricanes come ashore, they tend to move wooden structures into the second row, boats even farther.

After taking my boat, *Daddy's Girl*, inland, I returned to the Grand Strand to find Chad brimming with excitement.

"We're going to a hurricane party."

"Not interested."

"Suze, you've been to one. I want that experience."

"I don't think so." Glancing around the landing, I saw that most of the boats were gone.

My berth mate, Harry Poinsett, and I had already sailed southward and inland, as most hurricanes come ashore and move northward. It had been a real traffic jam of river craft pushing into the wind and rain. Everyone along the Grand Strand remembered Hugo. Everyone but my boyfriend, it would appear.

Chad's invite was to weather the storm in a house that had been built in Victorian style just after the Second World War: three stories, gables, two staircases, one a spiral, and ten-foot ceilings. It had a wraparound porch, fifteen rooms, five to each floor, and some of the most beautiful furniture I had ever seen.

Ever since I'd gotten it through my thick head that Chad Rivers really loved me, I'd bent over backwards to make our relationship work. This time though, as I pedaled along in the wind and the rain, I felt I was meeting him more than halfway, and it really chapped me.

When Chad and I arrived, people were busily shuttering the place. One car, a yellow Nissan sedan, sat in the crushed shell parking lot behind the house. As we rode up on our bicycles, a young redhead I recognized ran down the steps and into the parking area. The girl, now in her twenties, was someone I had once gone looking for during the early days of my searching for runaways along the Grand Strand.

She was in tears as she rushed to her car and kept chanting, "I can't do this! I can't do this!" She hopped in the yellow Nissan and was out of there.

"Need I say more?" I asked, turning to Chad as rain hit me in the face.

He gave a snort of disgust.

A bearded guy wearing a yellow slicker straightened up from where he stood near an opening under the house. The foundation of the house was made of concrete, awash with sand, and about three-feet high.

After watching the redhead go, he waved us over and raised his voice over the sound of the wind. "There's chains under here for your bikes."

Chad and I locked up our bikes alongside several others under the house, then wandered around to where we had seen two guys moving a ladder from one second-story window to another. Chad said the house had plenty of tongue-and-groove lumber throughout and hurricane straps holding the trusses together. He said it had been built to withstand hurricanes.

Yeah, right.

With a hurricane you're most concerned about shutters and escape routes. Since none of us was smart enough to leave the beach area, that meant we'd be worried about shutters, along with provisions once the storm had passed. Nothing much works once a hurricane passes through, and all the stores would have already been emptied of food, lumber, and purified water. I intended to check our host's provisions. I did not want to be dependent on what I'd hauled in on my bike and my back.

Victorian-style homes don't usually have shutters, but this is the Grand Strand, so there's always a likelihood of storms. Black galvanized steel shutters had been added, and unlike most add-ons, these actually worked. The paint had been baked on at the factory.

On the ground floor the shutters had been easily secured. The second story was a bit dicier. A guy wearing a camouflage poncho and baseball cap gripped the top of a twenty-foot ladder, held at its base by two other men. An "oops!" by one of them holding the ladder sent Chad tossing his pack on the wraparound porch and running to their assistance. I clutched my backpack and shook my head. I truly did love this guy and I could only hope I wouldn't pay for my devotion.

The one with the billowing poncho held two steel rods in his free hand; with the other he clutched the top of the ladder. Very quickly he reached up and placed one rod across hooks already in place on opposite sides of the closed shutters. The other rod he dropped across a pair of matching hooks at the bottom.

The guy in the billowing camouflage poncho was up and down the ladder in less than a minute. While his helpers, now including Chad, moved the ladder, the climber jerked down tightly on the bill of his baseball cap, picked up two more steel rods, and returned to the base of the ladder. They'd repeated this routine on all four sides of the house.

Swallowing my annoyance, I headed in the direction of the crushed shell parking lot and found the guy in the yellow slicker hauling a sheet of half-inch plywood from under the house. The wind didn't make this easy so I dumped my pack on the porch, caught up with him, and grabbed one end of the rectangular-shaped piece of wood.

He smiled in appreciation, and we carried the board over and placed it against the door where I'd seen the redhead exit. As I held it against the door, the guy with the beard looked for where the predrilled holes in the plywood matched the holes in the frame of the house.

"Upside down," he informed me. On this side of the house facing the road you didn't have to shout.

We flipped the board over, and almost lost the sucker in a gust of wind. The guy caught his end before it whopped him up against the head.

"Thanks again," he said with a nervous grin.

He let go of the board, put a shoulder into it, and slipped his free hand under the slicker, reaching into his jeans' pocket. Out came the screws, and from his back pocket he produced a Phillips head screwdriver and went to work fitting the screws through the holes while I held the board against the door. Matching the holes was tricky, but once he had one screw inserted and a second diagonally across from it, he fitted the rest easily in place. Now the rear entrance of the house was secured.

After slipping the Phillips under his slicker, he extended a hand. "Jeremy Knapp." He regarded me with his soft, brown eyes. His round, tanned face was partly hidden under the hood of his yellow slicker and the beard. "Didn't you hang around the Pavilion?"

I took his extended hand. "Susan Chase, and it was The Attic." A place where teens hang to get away from their parents and vice-versa.

"Now I remember. The girl who loved to dance. Didn't know there were going to be any girls at the party except for the witch."

What he said threw me off my stride and I entirely forgot about the redheaded female. "The witch?"

"Lady Light. You know, the witch on the Web. She's going to make the hurricane go away."

I looked in the direction of the storm. The three-story

structure sat on a point with breakers running from a sand beach. Now there was no beach and you could barely see the craggy rocks that formed the jetty that protected the point. Thick gray clouds lay low above a dark and angry sea, palm trees leaned in a wind that often changed direction, and oily-looking waves crashed ashore.

"Then I wish her luck."

"That's why I'm here. Two experiences for the price of one."

"Pardon me?"

"I've never attended a hurricane party."

"So I figured."

"You went through a hurricane?"

"Yes, but I was very drunk."

"What was it like?"

"Don't let me spoil your fun."

He looked at the churning seas less than a hundred feet from where we stood. "Think we're in any real danger?"

"That has a certain appeal to you?"

"I don't want to die. I'm like anyone else."

"Anyone else left days ago."

"Why didn't you?"

"I'm with that guy over there."

I gestured at the guy with the blond hair and terrific-looking shoulders, who, with a skinny guy dressed in black, brought the ladder around the house. As we watched, the ladder was rested on hooks on the back wall that snapped over, trapping the ladder in place.

"You're with Chad?" asked Jeremy Knapp.

I nodded as my fiancé and his new friend disappeared around the front of the house.

Jeremy smiled. "Standing by your man?"

I shrugged. "What did you mean about two experiences for the price of one?"

We were still behind the house where the diminished sounds of the wind and surf made it easier to speak. Still, the rain had the nasty habit of sneaking under the bill of my baseball cap and tattooing my face.

"My mother and father had government jobs and they hated them," he said. "Their parents had drummed into their heads what it had been like living through the Great Depression, so my folks opted to work for Uncle Sam." He laughed. "My brother and sister both have government jobs they hate."

"And a pretty good retirement plan."

He regarded me as we rounded the corner of the house and headed for the wraparound porch. "And what do you do for a living, if I might ask?"

"Professional lifeguard."

"Yeah," he said, raising his voice, "if I remember correctly, you always had a great tan."

I didn't mention my job with SLED because some people don't care to have cops at parties, and several times I've had to ask Chad to leave because of what people were doing, or what they wanted us to do. But there was no way we could leave this party, so Chad and I'd agreed I would use the story of my former career as a lifeguard and runaway finder.

"Susan, I've been up the Amazon, ridden on the Orient Express since they've gotten it up running again, and traveled to the North Pole."

I could only stop and stare, then follow that with a "Wow!" Glimmers of what I could do if I wasn't engaged flashed through my head.

"My brother and sister put me down because they're jealous of what I've done."

"Accomplished."

He shook his head as we trudged through the rain. "According to my parents I haven't accomplished anything. I got hooked on Marco Polo when I was a kid and used to hitch up and down the East Coast. It's more than a kid's game played in swimming pools. Did you know that Marco Polo spent years in the Far East working for the emperor and mastered several languages?"

"And how many languages have you mastered on all your jaunts?"

"Mastered?" He stopped. "Why would I? Everyone speaks English."

"What's your connection to Lady Light?" Lady Light, or Helen McCuen, had not been mentioned when Chad had brought up the subject of attending a hurricane party.

"Connection?" He was more guarded now. As we continued toward the steps of the wraparound porch, he asked, "What do you mean?"

"My boyfriend was invited, probably because he and Helen attended the same high school. I imagined you knew Lady Light from a past life."

"Helen and I met at Carolina." Meaning the University of South Carolina, or the real USC, as it is called in these parts.

"You were collecting the experience of being Joe College?"

"Never finished. Just trying to please my parents. Lady Light was studying broadcast journalism; me, the traditional print stuff. We used to argue about who'd have the greatest impact on society. She wanted to be the next Jane Pauley. Then, the summer before her senior year she interned at a local TV station. When she saw all the backstabbing and turf wars that go on behind the scenes, she opted to move to Hollywood and become a movie star. If she was going to go through all that garbage, she might as well make a run at the brass ring. It sounded like a pretty cool gig, so she and

I spent a couple of years in L.A. trying to break into the movies."

"I take it that didn't work out."

He shook his head and rain fell from the hood of his yellow slicker as he went up the side steps. "Out there, blondes are a dime a dozen, and me, I don't have the looks. No cheekbones." He picked up my pack and I let him. "But I had the chance to travel to Hawaii and up the Pacific Coast." He glanced out to sea. "You know, they have an entirely different beach up there."

"I've heard there's none."

"You'd be pretty close to correct. I've kept up with Lady Light through her web site. She got into witchcraft about the same time I left for Alaska."

"Summer or winter visit?" I asked with a smile.

"I've done both," he said with a smirk.

"So you asked to come to the party."

"Pretty much. I spent last spring chasing tornadoes."

"Like in the movie *Twister.*"

"Just like that," he said with a nod.

Chad and the other three men huddled at the front door, somewhat protected by the porch. Water dripped from their rain gear and puddled at their feet. If the hurricane came ashore there would be more than puddles on this porch.

Chad flashed me a smile as we approached the additional members of the party, and I tried to return the smile but failed miserably. Behind him, the shutters for the double doors were still open, hooked in place, waiting for the last person to go inside.

Before we reached the others, I asked, "When you think you'll settle down?"

Jeremy looked at me. "Now you sound like my mother."

"Just making conversation. We're not going anywhere soon." I took my pack from him as the ocean slammed into shore. The wind had really gotten up, and the rain came at us on the horizontal. I turned away from the stinging drops.

"Maybe I'll find a woman who likes to travel." He stopped before we reached the others, and that had the intended result. I stopped, too, and my wet Nikes squeaked on the wet surface of the porch. "What about you?" he asked. "Like to tag along?"

"Not a chance," I said, extending the hand with the engagement ring. Water dripped from my finger and made the rock glisten. "I have to make sure my invitations go out."

"Sorry to hear that, Susan."

"I'm not."

He glanced at Chad, who had pulled back the top of his rain gear. "So you'll marry, have the house, the kids, and the picket fence—that appeals to you?"

"I'm an orphan, Jeremy. Any kind of family appeals to me."

"With no ties to the community, you could take off anytime."

"I'd lose my job."

"It's not much of a job, but that's not my point."

"Your point is that I should have the same interest in roaming the globe as you do. It's like parents who give their kids weird names—because no one ever made fun of their names while growing up, why not give their kid a zippy-sounding name. You couldn't understand the attraction of having a family because you've always had a mother, father, and that brother and sister you blow off."

He laughed before heading for the group standing near the front doors. "This is going to be an interesting party."

"It's an oxymoron to call a hurricane party a 'party.'"

"You think we're all nuts."

"Before this is over, you'll all think you're nuts."

Chapter 2

Three guys stood on the porch with Chad. The one wearing a Tommy Hilfiger rain jacket and dark, fashionable boots was shorter than my five-foot-ten, and lots heavier. Jeremy introduced us, though it was unnecessary. Reynolds Pearce was an investment banker from Charlotte and another guy I knew from dancing at The Attic. A groper.

Reynolds didn't look at me, only nodded and continued to stare at the ocean. "I don't see how she's—"

Jeremy interrupted him. "You, of all people, have more reason to believe that Lady Light can do this."

"Still, I just don't see how anyone is going to be able to stop that storm."

"You'll see," said Jeremy with a knowing smile.

Reynolds nodded and continued to stare at the storm.

It was difficult to keep your eyes off the surf washing over the jetty, chunks of rocks extending into the ocean. After washing over them, the surf crashed into the berm, and occasionally a stand of sea oats would be flattened against the sand by the wind.

"This is better than any damn game," muttered the tall skinny guy who had helped Chad bring the ladder around to the rear of the house. Brandon Calhoun wore black hair to his shoulders and a black hat in the style of that worn by Indiana Jones. His long raincoat was the same color, as were his jeans.

I'd seen Brandon Calhoun on the streets of Myrtle Beach LARPing, or live action role-playing, using the Grand Strand for the backdrop of his games. Live action role-players really get into their characters, which have a tendency toward vampirism. You can imagine the shock of some poor soccer mom, and her kids, caught in the middle of a game as LARPS go about their business of searching for the missing touchstone or some such garbage.

Brandon would make a good vampire. Hollow cheeks, and long, narrow nose. When he opened his mouth, you could see where his incisors had been filed into points. His face was pale, which is something you really have to work at when you live at the beach.

"Game?" asked Reynolds, who'd apparently just met his first LARPer.

Brandon told Reynolds what he did for amusement, and Reynolds looked at Brandon as if learning an adult was still playing in a Pokémon league.

Reynolds and Chad exchanged glances over Brandon's shoulders. Chad shrugged.

The other man was bald-headed with a pockmarked face, broad shoulders, large hands, and a thick neck. Sarge was actually Perry Jackson, a former buck sergeant who had served during Operation Desert Storm, as I would later learn. Besides the camouflage poncho and baseball cap with an American flag on the front, Sarge's hair was cut in a buzz. I don't think Sarge had gotten the military complex completely out of his system.

"You here to protect us, Perry?" I'm not much into being protected, and many a time that has been a burr under my fiancé's saddle. Perry Jackson was so unlike the others I could not imagine that he would know them on anything more than a professional basis. But he did, and that was something else I didn't learn right away.

"It's what I was hired to do, Miss—I didn't catch your name."

"Chase. Susan Chase. Someone hired you?"

"My orders are to make sure the house is secure, that no one's tinkered with anything."

"Why would they do that?"

"Lady Light has had death threats."

"Because she's going to try to stop the hurricane?"

My bearded friend filled me in. "There are those who think wiccans shouldn't interfere with the forces of nature."

"Wiccans?" asked Chad.

"Witches," I tossed off. To Jeremy I said, "It was my impression that wiccans and other pagans believe they're in tune with nature like no one else."

"I wasn't expecting you, Miss Chase," continued the former sergeant, "but now that Miss Archibald's left there's provisions enough—"

A high-pitched yelp from behind the house drew our attention in that direction. We all hustled around the corner to the end of the wraparound porch. The body of a woman lay face down in the shell parking area. Hooked on each arm was a plastic bag from BiLo at the Beach, a local grocery chain, and beside her lay a bicycle. Through the light-brown plastic bags, we could see multicolored sacks and packages.

Chad scrambled down the steps and reached her first, and when he did, the woman's head was already raised, an embarrassed grin on her face. Apparently she had tripped when dismounting her bike with all her packages and ended up in a puddle; otherwise, there would have been no such grin. And if not for her poncho—which was clear—she would have gotten her clothing soaked.

As Chad helped to her feet, I, as well as the men, could see she had an ample chest, a tiny waist, and legs with curves even her tan cargo shorts couldn't hide. Chad was trying to free the plastic bags tangled around the woman's arms when she out-and-out threw her arms, and the grocery bags, around him and gave him a big, fat kiss.

"My hero once again" were the words that floated on the wind in my direction.

I was ready to charge down the stairs, but motivated by higher levels of testosterone, the males beat me to her. I took a first step down, thought better about it, and returned to the porch, glaring.

Chad, to his credit, was trying to extricate himself from the shapely woman's hold. With some assistance from the others, the bags were disentangled from her arms, and she was escorted to the steps, then up on the porch, Chad on one side, Jeremy on the other.

I stood with feet spread and arms across my chest, engagement ring glistening in the rain, saying nothing.

"That was very sweet of you," I heard her say upon reaching the porch and throwing back the hood of her poncho. She stood on tiptoes to give Chad another kiss, this one a peck on the cheek.

Chad flushed. "Vicki, I'd like you to meet my fiancée. This is Susan."

The girl glanced at my face, then took in the engagement ring on my wet hand.

Words tumbled out of her mouth as her hand fell away. "Oh, I'm so sorry. I didn't mean to embarrass you." Vicki turned her attention to me. "I'm Vicki Hester and Chad *was* my hero. He had to get my car started more than once on the way to school. We lived along the same road. I drove a clunker. Chad drove his . . ."

Her voice trailed off. Hester was looking at the other men, most who would not meet her eyes. "Chad's fiancée was invited to the party?"

Neither Chad nor anyone else said anything. Uh-huh. Soon my main man was going to be filling me in, and on a lot more than the my-hero-again B.S.

Hester gestured at the grocery sacks the guys were holding and flashed a big smile. "No way I'm eating all that nutritious stuff Helen has planned. After all," she added, giving me a meaningful look, taken to mean that any gal with good sense would get on her horse and ride out of here, "we could all die here."

But I wasn't a gal with good sense. I was in love, and standing by my man. That made me ask, "Sarge, I didn't see your vehicle in the parking lot."

The former soldier had returned from chaining Vicki Hester's bike under the house. "It wasn't part of the original contract, but I'm not comfortable leaving . . ." he glanced at Vicki Hester ". . . with all you being here."

"You're staying to protect the women and children."

"There are no children, Miss Chase."

I inclined my head in the direction of the men holding the grocery bags.

"What I'm saying, Miss Chase, is my expertise should be available if things get out of hand."

"Like a hurricane leveling this house?"

He turned his buzz-shaven head to scan the porch of the gabled structure, then walked in the direction of the front of the house. We all trailed along.

"I don't think there's much chance of that, the way this place is built. You'd have to be in the middle of the strike zone."

"We may end up in the strike zone," said Reynolds Pearce, trailing us to the corner overlooking the ocean, "if that witch goes toe-to-toe with this storm."

Waves were at eight feet, the horizon was a gray sheet of rain, and the dark clouds overhead had thickened and darkened. Rain slapped us in the face and someone suggested it might be a good idea to go inside.

There were murmurs of astonishment as something flew by. Paper, plastic, and Styrofoam were the usual items, but there was the occasional garbage can lid or lawn chair.

"Good God!" exclaimed Reynolds as he watched a seagull hurled past our line of sight.

We stepped forward and watched the bird disappear in the tangle of palms across the inlet from us. For our trouble we got more rain in our faces.

Along most stretches of the overdeveloped Grand Strand, homes of brick and mortar or homes built of wood might flank your house, but the owner of this house valued his privacy. The property had been cut out of an area well off the beach and the vegetation left to grow up around the three-story house.

"Who was the girl who left?" I asked.

"Wendy," offered our experience collector, Jeremy. He went on to explain that her grandmother owned the house, and whenever the grandmother went up north for the summer, a season that usually lingers into September in the Carolinas, she paid Wendy a hundred dollars a month to make sure the house was maintained. "And another three hundred if no one else stays in the house with her."

"Then we don't have permission to be here?" At this point I was looking for any way out.

"You have permission, Miss Chase," said Sarge. "My home office checked. Lady Light rented the house for the fall."

"For the hurricane season, you mean," I said, looking at my fiancé.

"What was Wendy so upset about?" asked Chad, his eyes flickering from me to our experience collector.

"She's not ready to be a witch," explained Jeremy. "Did you see her ponytail?"

Chad nodded.

"Witches never put their hair up or braid it. They always wear their hair loose and long-flowing, unless it interferes with their day job."

"Wendy did have a day job." When everyone looked at me, I added, "She was running for her life."

It seemed ridiculous that less than two weeks earlier, the storm didn't even have a name. Nobody knew about it, not even the National Hurricane Center. Still, something had occurred off the coast of Africa. The ocean had been lazing around, and when the ocean becomes lazy, it's at its most dangerous.

A lazy ocean has no fronts, and when you watch the Weather Channel, you see all sorts of fronts passing across the States almost daily. Fronts rubbing against each other over Kansas can become a tornado. Just the opposite happens along the equator. There, when nothing happens, it's a good chance a tropical disturbance will be born.

Ten to twenty degrees north of the equator, and with no fronts to change the water temperature, heated air begins to rise. This creates a vacuum, and every school child knows how Mother Nature feels about vacuums.

Hot, moist air fills that vacuum, and if enough moisture is sucked into the vacuum, it can, with the rotation of the earth, begin a counterclockwise motion. Heavy air in the center of the low-pressure area will be sucked upward and flung out of this invisible tube. Another lesson from your school days: Stuff that goes up must come down.

At higher altitudes, the air cools and the moisture falls as rain. To form a hurricane, the rain must fall ahead of the developing storm, and only when the trade winds give it a nudge does it threaten us. And once the storm begins its westerly jaunt, there's nothing between the storm and the beaches of the Grand Strand.

What Myrtle Beach needed was a Bermuda high lying south of the storm. If a Bermuda high was on station, Lili might cross the Caribbean into the Gulf. So golfers came to Myrtle Beach—their reservations made months before—along with the accompanying hookers. That was when Helen McCuen, a.k.a., the witch, broadcast on her Web site that if the disturbance threatened the coast, she would be there to match wits with the storm. Witchcraft versus natural phenomenon. A certain grabber for today's short attention spans.

A palmetto tree caught our attention as it became uprooted, tumbled across the yard, and came to rest against one of our own trees drowning in a half a foot of water. The uprooted palmetto—low-growing, fan-leaved palm trees populating the Grand Strand—wasn't there long. The wind changed direction, and up went the tree, soaring toward the angry, gray clouds. When the wind died, the palm fell toward the sea. But the wind returned off the ocean and sent the palm soaring—straight for us. For seconds we stood, gaping, then Sarge shouted, "Hit the deck."

We did as the tree slammed into one of the posts. The post snapped, and everyone went scrambling in opposite directions, slipping and sliding across the wet porch.

Looking up from where I lay with Chad's arm around me, I saw the shattered post. As for the palmetto, it had come to rest in a flowerbed below the railing, one of its many fronds flapping through the railing in a helpless gesture for assistance.

Turning to Chad, I said, "That redhead who left."

"Wendy?"

"She was right. All of us should be running for our lives."

Chapter 3

I remember Lady Light before she saw the light. She was Helen McCuen and just another upper-middle class girl growing up along the Grand Strand. Helen had guarded the beach as a teen, and then began to view lifeguarding with disdain, since so much riff-raff was working the trade. That meant me.

At fifteen, I was orphaned when my father, drunk again, fell off our family shrimp boat and drowned. Dear ol' Mom had already walked out on what was left of our family when I was thirteen. Before that I'd had two older siblings, but Sis overdosed in one of the gardens of good and evil in Savannah and my older brother was killed when a car lost one of its tires and came hurtling into the pit at Daytona where he was crewing. They said my brother never knew what hit him. The same might be said of Sis.

So I grew up with somewhat of an attitude, lacking all the social graces and respecting none. Fortunately for me, my berth mate at the marina, Harry Poinsett, was there, and if I have any clue to life's big picture, I have Harry Poinsett to thank for it. And my somewhat stilted prose. Harry says I'm stuck between being a permanent teenager and almost an adult. Whatever that means.

From the age of fifteen I raised myself, lifeguarding during the season, living by my wits the rest of the year. It took only one long, cold winter to learn I'd better sock some of that money away for those long winters when restaurants turn away girls like me who spend their summers sitting on a throne and being ogled by guys. Helen McCuen, however, had the poise, looks, and height to graduate to modeling, and she traveled as far as L.A. making the kind of money I could only envy. Still, I was the one who'd been there the night Helen lost her poise.

It had been a long, hot day guarding the beach, and I was about to meet with a parent searching for his runaway daughter. She had not exactly run away from home—she disappeared so she wouldn't have to return to Buffalo. You know the joke: Buffalo's not the end of the world, but you can see it from there. Her father had remained behind, which was a very good sign.

"This will take some time," I told the middle-aged man with the long face. He was waiting for me at a bar on Kings Highway, just a couple of blocks off the beach.

Before even taking a seat, I asked my client to order me a beer, and then I ducked into the rest room where I could change into street clothes. Swimsuits begin to chafe after a while. I returned to the table to find the waitress expecting some ID. I gave her a fake one and took a seat across the table from the man with the long face.

Several color photographs lay on the table between us. A wholesome family of five. I was interested in the freckled-faced teenager with the peeling sunburn. After noting the particulars, such as age, height, weight, on the back of one of the photographs, I asked what his daughter had found exciting about the Grand Strand.

He told me what he remembered, and this guy remembered a lot. Another good sign. I don't turn every kid over to their folks. Some parents have to pick them up at Child Protective Services.

He nodded nervously. "But you will find her?"

"I usually do." In those days I spoke with a confidence that, viewed today, makes me slightly nervous.

And why were we meeting at a bar? It was the closest place I could down a tall cool one, and with a hundred-dollar advance and a recommendation from the Myrtle Beach Police for finding runaway teens, I was ready to go. The trail was hot and I wanted to close the deal. I also wanted to buy an old pink jeep I'd seen for sale, and I didn't have the down payment.

I'd grown tired of hitching rides from where *Daddy's Girl* was moored. Wacca Wache Landing is on the Intracoastal Waterway, a series of bays, inlets, rivers, and ditches cleared by the Army Corps of Engineers so amateur sailors can sail all the way from Boston to Miami without ever having to put to sea. Wacca Wache is near Murrells Inlet, or the southern end of the Strand, and each morning I had to be up early and ready to go, hitching out to Kings Highway to catch a ride. One morning I climbed into the car with the wrong guy and had to fight my way out of there. That was why I was so eager to knock down some quick cash and make the down payment on that jeep.

With photo in hand, I finished the beer, left the bar, and struck out for the spots that had turned this kid on. Most of them were located along The Strip, that portion of the beach within a few blocks of the arcade. The Pavilion would be my first stop. The father said he'd had to drag his daughter out of there.

Music blared from cars along The Strip as the traffic edged along. Whoops and hollers came from those enjoying the night. And, yes, it bugged me that I wasn't dancing the night away, but I really wanted that jeep.

On my way to the bright lights, I spotted Helen McCuen in a parking lot. She was fighting off a guy who had his hands all over her.

"Stop that!" she yelled, her voice hardly audible over the noise from The Strip. "Stop it right now!" Her blouse was open, and the guy was wrestling to free her breasts from her bra.

I happened to see what was going on only because I was looking for the runaway. Runaways like to hang in parking lots near the Pavilion, smoking and joking, buying drugs, strutting their stuff. If they only knew how easy they were to find, or imitate.

I sauntered over to the confrontation. Helen was being held against a pickup by a hairy forearm under her chin. A small black purse lay on the asphalt and one of her sandals had fallen off.

"How about a threesome?" I asked, my back pack sliding off my shoulder and into my hand.

The lug looked at me, his arm came off Helen's throat, and he stopped fondling her boobs. Helen tucked her breasts back in their cups and started buttoning her blouse. Even in the semidarkness the guy's fresh sunburn was evident. He was a tourist looking for a little action—which I was more than ready to give him. Like I said, back then I believed I was invincible.

"This ain't none of your business." From the guy's tank top I could see he worked out, and had a chest only a woman who could tolerate lots of hair.

Out of the corner of my eye, I saw that Helen had picked up her purse and fitted back on her lost sandal.

"Helen, why don't you and I go somewhere you can buy me a drink?"

The lug stepped toward me. "You some kind of a tough guy."

"A guy? Nah. I'd never stoop that low."

My backpack fell from my hand as Helen hastily stuffed her silk blouse into her short-shorts. Nice outfit. Atlanta or New York. Certainly not something you'd find at Myrtle Beach, unless the labels had been cut out.

The guy reached for me, and I accommodated him by stepping inside his hands and jabbing him in the throat with the edge of my fingers. He stumbled away, bent over, and tried to catch his breath. His free hand flailed around for something to grab hold off.

While he was off balance, I kicked him in the hip with my foot and sent him sprawling. He lay on the ground more concerned with catching his breath—until I brought out my lifeguard whistle. Those days I always kept my whistle handy, in a small pouch Velcroed together at the top of my backpack. By then, Helen and I were on the sidewalk and leaving the parking lot behind. When the cops arrived—their reaction time during tourist season is like a flash of lightning before an approaching storm—Helen and I had blended in with the mob moving in the direction of the Pavilion.

She cleared her throat and brushed back her hair. "Thanks for what you did back there."

"No problema."

At a stall where baseball caps are sold, Helen checked her makeup in the mirror. Out came a hairbrush and she went to work on her long blond hair. Then she adjusted her lipstick, and after the damage was repaired, we headed off again down Ocean Boulevard.

"Er—how do you know my name?" she asked.

"First year I guarded the beach was the last year you worked for Marvin Valente."

"What's your name?"

"Susan Chase."

"Oh!" Her hand came up to her mouth. "I'm so sorry."

"Helen, you were younger then."

"But you—you were always much older than any of the other girls. That's probably why I picked on you."

"I thought it was some kind of initiation."

"Still, you have to understand that I was only mean to you because I was afraid of you."

"And me of you. And your crowd."

We walked along in silence until we stood across the street from the arcade, the Pavilion, and Ripley's Believe It or Not. Several cops gave me the eye, wondering what I might be up to. I'd seen that look before.

"Can I buy you that beer you mentioned?" asked Helen. "You have an ID, don't you?"

We entered a narrow hot dog joint facing the Strip. According to local lore, Peaches had been on that corner ever since the days when tourists were hauled in by wagon from Conway to enjoy a day at the beach. Once again, I had to flash my fake ID again, and to tell the truth, it was getting old not being twenty-one.

After the dogs arrived—mine with chili, Helen's receiving one line of mustard—she spoke again. You know, I've never figured how to eat a chili dog without getting chili all over me. If this'd been a date, I would've opted for something along the condiment Helen was using, but I love chili dogs, and there was nary a boyfriend in sight. I sighed. Perhaps I was putting too much value on that pink jeep.

"I never could've done something like you did back in that alley."

"You would've called the cops. Same difference." I was busy fitting the chilidog into my mouth. When I looked up, I found Helen staring at me.

"What?" I asked, straightening my spine and posture. "What?"

"You're blowing off what you did back there?"

"What were you doing in that alley anyway?"

She glanced around, then lowered her voice. "Trying to score some coke." A tentative smile, then: "It's the only food group models can enjoy."

Chewing my way through the greasy mess dripping into the palm of my hand, I nodded. "That's guys' new line, instead of asking you to come up and view their etchings."

Helen had learned to nibble her dog without messing up her lipstick. "Aren't you worried he might come looking for you?"

"Nah. He's only here for the week."

She focused on me again. "You know all the jerks along the Grand Strand?"

"Pretty much."

The next time I saw Helen she was so drunk she couldn't stand without wobbling. Worse, she was trying to open the door of a red BMW Roadster. Using the remote, the best Helen could do was lock herself out, pop the trunk, and activate the alarm. That brought a cop on the run. I saw him heading in Helen's direction, so I made a U-turn in the middle of the street with my new jeep and double-parked alongside her vehicle.

A tanned girl in a white cropped top and dark shorts laughed at Helen's ineptitude from the passenger side of the Roadster. When she saw the cop headed in their direction, she stumbled across the street and disappeared into the darkness of the Pavilion parking garage. I almost ran the girl down making my Bat turn.

Helen teetered even more precariously on a pair of black high heels. Besides the heels, she wore tan shorts that would give you a wedgie and a black silk blouse. Gold jewelry.

She smiled a crooked little grin that took away none of her charm. "Susan Chase, I do believe."

In a stern voice I informed her that the cops were on the way and that, under the circumstances, she'd better let me do the talking.

She looked behind her as the cop—he was black—slowed to a walk, sizing us up. His flashlight came out as he wandered over to us.

"What's the problem?" he asked as I finally got the horn to stop its incessant honking by working the remote and the key. I don't know which. I hadn't advanced to this sort of luxury.

"She called me," I explained, "but I got hung up."

"Called you for what?"

To keep Helen from falling on her face took both hands, so I gestured with my head at the pink jeep parallel-parked alongside the Roadster. We were on the wide sidewalk next to the rides of the Pavilion and across from the parking garage. The streets were empty, the rides shut down for the night, and the lights of the shops barely reached across the street.

"I got here as fast as I could, but I was held up at work."

"Work? Where's that?"

"I work for Marvin Valente."

"You're up pretty late for a lifeguard."

The cop used his light to check his watch. When he did, I saw that the name on the silver identity badge read "DeShields," and he wasn't all that bad looking. Next his light fell on me, and I twisted away from the brightness.

"It's almost midnight," he asked. "What were you doing at this hour of the night?"

"Checking the guard houses." Meaning the places where the out-of-town college kids are stashed while they save money from their summer of lifeguarding at Myrtle Beach. "Marvin heard more than sleeping was going on. I made a surprise visit."

The cop looked me over. I wore a pair of faded overalls, a sleeveless tee, and running shoes. My blondish hair was pulled back in a ponytail, and in truth, I had just left the clutches of a guy who thought groping was part of slow dancing. Sometimes I wonder why I make the effort. The next one who comes along is always a jerk.

"Maybe I'd better check your story." The light now moved to Helen.

"Yeah," I said, moving away and taking the tall, slender blonde with me. "Why don't you?" I gave him Marvin's number. "I'm sure my boss won't mind being called in the middle of the night." I carefully walked Helen around to the passenger side of the jeep. The image of his flashlight was a yellow spot in my vision. "He has to be up by five."

DeShields followed us, using his light. "I might have to arrest your friend for public intoxication."

As I sat Helen in the jeep, she took this moment to straighten up and say, "I am not drunk." Which slurred as the words came out, proving she was.

After making sure Helen was settled in her seat, I faced the cop. "What's the problem? Haven't met your quota?"

"Watch your mouth, kid."

"But we're not acting like kids. My friend has had too much to drink, she called me, and I'm going to take her home. I'm her designated driver."

"Then touch your nose."

"What?"

"Either touch your nose and prove you're not drunk or I'm taking you both in."

Hey, I can be as tough as the next gal, but that would only end up with Helen in the drunk tank. So I touched my nose and let him pass his finger back and forth in front of my eyes. After following the finger, and resisting the urge to give him one, I did a one-legged stand without being asked and began saying the alphabet rapidly.

"It appears you know the drill," grumbled DeShields.

"I grew up along the Strand. I know what cops do to pass the time when their shift begins to drag."

"Listen here, kid—"

Our repartee was interrupted when Helen leaned out of my Jeep and puked up the slice of pizza she'd had for dinner. White foam with reddish-brown chunks sprayed the asphalt near the feet of the cop.

"Damn!" DeShields jumped back. "I just bought these shoes."

Needless to say I didn't have to finish the test.

After making sure Helen's car was secure, I took her home to *Daddy's Girl*, the old shrimp boat I live on. I got her into the lower bunk after stripping her and washing her upper body with a warm, soapy washcloth. And yeah, I couldn't help but notice that Helen had the perfect body for modeling: tall, leggy, and without much hint of bosom or butt.

I stripped to my underpants, washed off the odor, and

then pulled on a tee and sacked out in the upper bunk. I had to be up early while Helen would be sleeping in.

She was still zonked out when I dragged myself out of bed at six—damn that alarm clock Marvin bought for me—pulled on my swimsuit, washed my face, and brushed back my hair. Then I grabbed my backpack and was out the door with a Pepsi and a Pop-tart. Before I left, I scribbled a note that said her sports car was parked out front and the keys were with my berth mate, Harry Poinsett.

She came looking for me and found me around noon.

"What the hell was that all about?" she demanded from the foot of my throne. I noticed Helen wore the same clothes as the night before, but she had her high heels in her hand to negotiate the sand out to my throne.

Up and down the beach, tourists were sunning on towels, others lay in chairs under umbrellas, rented or otherwise. Music played on both sides of my lifeguard stand: one radio playing rock, the other, country. The ocean was dark and blue, a mild tide was receding from shore, and the sun was strong enough to require glasses. There was little or no breeze.

"My parents were worried sick," she shouted up at me. "The least you could've done was to have called them."

"I didn't have their number."

"You could've speed-dialed it on my cell. It was in my purse."

Tourists rolled their heads in our direction, noses covered in zinc oxide in a variety of colors. Many of those faces were beginning to burn. That wasn't my business. I was responsible for those in the surf, and, it would appear, Helen McCuen.

"Helen, it didn't dawn on me to use your cell. I don't own one."

"Well, you should."

"And who would I call?"

Her face wrinkled up in anger. "Oh, you street people are impossible!"

She was gone a little over three hours. When she returned, I was putting away the equipment. To tell the truth, I didn't think I'd ever see her again, but when she pitched in putting away the umbrellas and chairs, I didn't object. Kids, hotties, lost girls helping out, who am I to complain?

Once the box was locked and the chairs wired together, Helen glanced at the sand. "I talked with Melinda Walters."

I said nothing.

"She saw . . ." Helen cleared her throat before going on. "She saw the whole thing from the parking garage across the street." She glanced away. "I've been to my father's office and home to see my mom. I've been grounded, but I'm able to go out one last time."

A blue credit card appeared from behind her back. "My father said I was to take you to dinner."

"Helen, I don't want anything from you."

"Susan, please don't make this any more difficult than it is."

Heading for my jeep, I said, "I really don't care what you or your folks think."

She came after me. "I'm only trying to make this right."

At the public access area between two motels, I faced her. "Helen, you and I come from different worlds. They just happened to become jammed. It won't happen again because the next time the guy will rape you or you'll end up in jail. That'll change your life more than any dinner date with me."

"But—but you can't go through life not connecting with people."

"What other choice do I have?"

"You could come with me tonight and have dinner on my dad." She glanced at her feet. "I can see you as often as I want. My father says . . ." She cleared her throat to finish. "My father says—er, I might learn a thing or two from you."

So we became chums of sorts and her parents wanted to meet me. Ironically, they ran in the same circle as the Rivers, the family of my future fiancé, though I didn't know it at the time. Helen's mother took one look at what I wore and decided to make me over.

I was having none of that. "Have any clothes you're about to toss out?"

Now that you mentioned it, said her mother, there were some things intended for Goodwill.

"That'll be good enough for me."

It didn't work, and not for Helen's lack of trying, or perhaps a desire to use the escape hatch her parents had given her. I didn't want to fit into her world.

Not until I met Chad Rivers.

A year later, we ran into each other and bought each other a beer. "How's the modeling trade?" I asked.

"I'll have plenty of money for my junior year."

"What you majoring in?" I had learned how to talk to these college types.

"Broadcast journalism. I intern at a TV station next summer. That's when it gets serious."

And she went on to tell me that those who studied

broadcast journalism had to endure what was called Senior Semester, in which the students have to put on a TV newscast on the local PBS affiliate.

Helen was aiming for one of the anchors' chairs, and with her looks, she just might get it. Unfortunately, that didn't work out. After all the backstabbing, turf wars, and politics she saw at the local affiliate, Helen opted for a shot at Hollywood, just as Jeremy Knapp had informed me.

"And your parents?" I asked the next time I ran into her.

This was several years later. You really had to wonder what they thought of their child becoming a witch while on the West Coast; and then again, maybe not. It's not called the Left Coast for nothing.

"My folks said they'd finance my shot at Hollywood for two years. After that I have to get a real job."

Jeez. Where do you find parents like that? Some even send their kids to Europe after college. I thought that only happened in old movies.

"In L.A. I found my way to the craft," Helen had said the last time I saw her. Later I heard that she was on the web preaching about how we should get in touch with Mother Earth. Mother Earth is very important to witches.

"Susan," she said over beers, "I realized how I grew up made me insensitive to the world around me."

No kidding.

She looked out the window of the Sea Captain, a seafood restaurant that would later be written up in *USA Today*. "Imagine growing up at the beach and not noticing the natural world. That's what I mean by having my senses dulled by the mundane world."

"Er—the mundane world would be the workaday

world we all live in?"

She nodded. "And why we have lost contact with Mother Earth."

"Helen—"

"Please, 'Lady Light.' "

"Whatever. You witches think the rest of us aren't in harmony with the . . . world."

"Correct," she said, sitting upright and not having lost one bit of her poise. Helen's hair was loose, over her shoulders. She wore lipstick but little other makeup. Her clothing was layered, the top a colorful cotton print overlaid by a smart-looking vest. Around her neck hung a necklace with a silver pendant featuring a triple moon. I didn't ask. True believers could go on and on.

"Er—Helen, what's wrong with meditation, or sitting on the beach and enjoying the sunset?"

"Nothing. I do that myself."

"But if a Christian—?"

"Christians usually pray."

"And you don't?"

"We attempt to stay in harmony with Mother Earth."

Which was where Helen ran into trouble. A lot of people think witches worship the devil, and you sure didn't want to be known as a devil worshiper in the state of South Carolina. That could get you into big trouble. That could get you killed.

Chapter 4

As the erratic storm called Lili moved toward the Grand Strand, it developed mass, but more importantly, increased its rhythm. Huge waves ahead of the storm rolled across the ocean, moving four to five times faster than the sea. The animals living along the coast sensed the warning and reacted accordingly. Humans glanced toward the sea, but it was only the animals that made plans for the future as the waves tumbled and thudded against reefs, rocks, and sand. Birds headed inland, away from the dropping air pressure, fish stored food for the days ahead, and fiddler crabs hustled inland, large claws held high. An odd sight, if you didn't understand the fiddler was scurrying for its life.

The interior of the house was gorgeous and elegant, nothing shabby like its worn and weather-beaten exterior. When we opened one of the double doors at the entrance of the house, we found ourselves in a vestibule no more than four feet deep, then we passed through another set of tall doors into a hall. To the left of the hallway was the living room, to the right, an alcove where we hung our coats and placed our wet footwear. Above that alcove, stairs wrapped around until they reached the second floor, which I really couldn't see from where we stood. But we could see down the shiny hardwood hallway and through another set of double doors. A door of the second set was open at the far end of the hall, presumably leading to the kitchen, and through that faraway opening, I noticed the base of another set of stairs, not nearly so grand.

However, I'm getting ahead of myself.

Sarge shouldered his way past both Vicki and myself with a lack of chivalry that surprised me. He stopped at the second set of doors and gave what could only be called a special knock. Not "shave and a haircut, two bits," but different from plain old knocking.

One of the two front doors opened and Helen McCuen welcomed us into her home. "Merry meet, all!"

Her appearance stopped me, and I stepped aside as others stumbled in from wind forcing its way through the vestibule. I could see a change come over everyone as they shook off the water, then shed their rain gear, and began to hang it in the alcove under the stairs.

Well, what the hell, outside they'd been subject to the elements. Here they were going to be subject to another set of elements, ones even I didn't understand.

A wide rubber mat lay on the floor to protect it from our wet footgear, and above that mat several short wooden pegs where we hung our outer garments. You could smell boots and shoes that needed a good airing, as well as several of the attendees, who'd worked hard in their slickers and ponchos to secure the exterior of the house. All that was quickly banished by the scent of incense from the living room.

"Susan, is that you?"

"'Tis me," I said, facing my one-time friend who stood

in the entranceway of the living room.

Helen McCuen still had her regal bearing and her long blond hair. Instead of fashionable clothing from Atlanta or New York, she wore a dark, long-sleeved dress, loosely gathered at her thin waist, that almost reached the floor. And a pair of silver earrings in the design of quarter moons.

Behind her, a red velvet sofa sat against the far wall. Flanking it were end tables with ornate lamps and several miniature portraits in gilt-edged frames. The coffee table was built low to the floor with four legs forming delicate "Ls." To my left sat two Queen Anne chairs with a small, round table between them. A brass floor lamp peered over the shoulder of one of the chairs.

Across the room from the sofa, and to my immediate right, two straight-backed chairs with upholstered seats appeared to have been hauled in just for the occasion. Behind the chairs stood a cabinet with glass doors and glass shelves that held dishes, glasses, and bowls from another era. The fifties. Or the thirties. Or Transylvania.

"Nice to see all of you again," said Helen to the assembled crowd. "Please join me in the living room. I have prepared drinks for all."

I followed the others into the living room where we were offered drinks from a bottle of white zinfandel. I gulped down mine before remembering it could contain a Mickey Finn. Glancing around, I saw that everyone had found a seat, and Helen was smiling after placing the wine bottle on the low coffee table. Jeremy sat in one of the Queen Anne chairs, and he gestured for me to take the other. I did. It felt good to be off my feet.

"Feel free to help yourself to more wine," Lady Light said, taking a seat in one of the two straight-backed chairs dragged in just for the occasion.

Over my shoulder the brass lamp peered, though its light was off. There was no electricity along the Grand Strand these days, and a candle flickered in its place, mounted in one of many glass holders scattered around the room. Straight across from where I sat hung a pair of humongous pocket doors in which panels rolled from the interiors of walls separating the two rooms. From the other side of those huge doors came the sound of a piano being played in minor chords. In the corner stood a three-inch-diameter bowl of fired clay atop a wrought iron tripod about eight inches high. From that bowl came swirling smoke and the odor of incense. With a stem that distinctly wound upwards, the glass I had recently emptied appeared to draw the red, orange, and yellow colors from the smoke or candles.

Truth be known, Helen McCuen didn't look like the weirdo I was afraid she'd become. She appeared to have the serenity and assurance of someone with nothing less than a black belt in witchcraft. I had to force myself to remember that I had previously met Helen on my terms, in the so-called workaday world. Here, however, the candles, the incense, and the music from whatever-the-hell-it-was being played, not to mention the wine, created an environment in which, I confess, I found relief from the storm. It was enough to make you buy into witchcraft, especially if you weren't smart enough to take shelter farther inland.

Jeremy Knapp got to his feet, crossed the room, and pushed back one, then the second, of the huge set of pocket doors between the living room and what I later came to know as the ritual room. Slowly, we got to our feet and followed him and Lady Light into the adjoining room.

It might've been a dining room or where someone had once performed on the oboe, but this afternoon there was nothing but a plain square table holding a horn, a seashell, and a single candle burning in another bowl molded by a potter. The walls of the room were in flickering shadows, but I could see that furniture had once been there and had been removed for the ceremony. On the floor under the table sat a glass bottle filled with a dark substance, and lying alongside it, a wooden staff about four feet long. There were other things I couldn't make out in the subdued light, but I was sure they would be shown to me in due time.

We were asked to gather in a circle around the table, Helen and Jeremy showing how to do it: man, woman, man. I was beginning to get the idea that Jeremy was some sort of witch himself. Chad took my hand, flashed a warm smile, and then took the hand of Vicki Hester. Completing the circle were Sarge, Reynolds, and Brandon. Then, as we stood there, Helen painted pentagrams on our foreheads with a sweet-smelling oil.

"In perfect love and trust we gather inside this circle," repeated Helen as she moved from one person to the other.

Finished, she returned to the table and stuck the glass stopper in the mouth of the bottle which she placed under the table again. "Please close your eyes and try to calm your breathing. If you can relax, we will all become one."

So we stood there and held hands. There was considerable heavy breathing, and once again, the sound of music being played in a minor chord on a piano that could not be seen, and the smell of incense drifting in from the living room. After a couple of minutes, I felt a bit drowsy. It had to be the wine.

When I was told I could open my eyes, I saw that Helen held the four-foot shaft with a huge white gemstone mounted at the top. She moved it around, appearing to mark her territory. I imagined this was what is called "casting the circle" because there are a lot of mentions of casting circles when you hang around a brand-new witch, as I had several years ago. The gem on the end of the shaft caught the candlelight, and around us the air seemed to glow. Still the corners of the room remained in darkness.

"Please repeat after me. I conjure this space . . ."

We dutifully repeated the beginning of the phrase.

". . . between worlds," went on Helen.

This, too, we repeated.

". . . we invoke the gods and goddesses to protect us."

How Lady Light was going to quiet the storm, I had no idea, but I was willing to buy into the concept. I didn't want another Hugo slamming into this coast. I'd lost friends in that storm and come close to losing my own life.

Lady Light moved to the corner of the table, or what appeared to be the edge of the bubble of light, where she faced east and raised her hand in salute to the eastern element. Each time she did this, she took something different from the floor under that particular edge of the table.

This salute to each element was repeated at the other three points of the compass, and each time she saluted that quarter of the earth, she had something different in her hands. When she faced east, it was a bird feather, south was a burning candle, west a silvery bowl filled with water, and north, a piece of driftwood. How appropriate. That might represent us later today.

What time was it? Things were becoming a bit fuzzy. Before noon, Chad and I had begun our journey toward the beach. Now it had to be . . . .

"Diana," intoned Helen, "we beseech thee to descend upon the body of your servant and priestess. See with her eyes, touch with her hand, kiss with her lips . . . Diana, we invite you to join us in this circle, to be present with us and protect us . . . ."

Suddenly, Helen appeared to stiffen, then relax. A smile warmed her face as she looked from one of us to the other. "Diana is with us and we are together."

The group, still holding hands, began to move clockwise. That was encouraging. Hurricanes move in the opposite direction. Maybe we did have a chance.

"Please repeat after me . . . 'We are a circle, within a circle, with no beginning, and no ending.' "

So we chanted this mantra as we moved clockwise, and the speed of our little band grew as we repeatedly rounded the table—until Lady Light stopped us at the adjoining door of the living room.

She held her gleaming staff—the light seemed to have grown with our little march—and moved the staff across, and down, creating a hole in the protective bubble so we could exit the circle surrounding the table and its candle.

I had a moment of panic. We were leaving the safe zone.

But I had nothing to worry about. Witches are very elemental. They feel at home whether in a rose garden or at a hurricane party.

Helen marched out of the ritual room, through the living room, and out the double doors and back onto wet front porch, then down the beach—and into the mouth of the storm, chanting all the way. Jeremy was left in the ritual room in care of the candle. Gee, why couldn't I've been chosen for that job?

Wind and rain hammered us. We weren't dressed for this and quickly became soaked. Still, with hair streaming down her head and clothing soaked, nothing broke Helen's concentration. She held center court as we formed a crescent around her on the near side of the berm. Our chanting continued, though sounding a bit strained at times, especially when a blast of air off the ocean tried to flatten us.

Facing the storm and holding high the gleaming staff which appeared to suck the remaining light from the sky, Helen said: "Oh, mighty Diana of the heavens. You who command the movements of the ocean tides. I, Lady Light, beseech you now, in this hour of our deepest need, to hear us. Grant me your power. Descend on the body of your priestess and servant. See with my eyes, hear with my ears, feel with my skin the power of your ocean."

Helen appeared to grow larger, the stone atop the staff appeared to glow, and I realized I was losing it.

Pointing the staff in the direction of the storm, she said, "I, Diana, queen of the heavens and queen of the seas, command you, Lili, to turn from this place. Return to the sea, my child."

I gulped. The light from the stone was blinding, or my eyes were fixed on the staff. The gemstone appeared to direct its light toward the storm, and our attention in that direction. For some reason, I didn't feel the wind in my hair, the rain on my face . . . I didn't feel anything for the longest time as our chanting continued and the light focused like a laser at the heart of the storm.

Then I was cold, and Helen lay motionless in the wet grass at our feet.

Chad knelt beside her, scooping her up. "Helen, are you all right?"

We all stared at the woman in his arms. The staff lay beside her, no longer glowing. The glow was behind us. The waters began to calm, the wind died down, and the rain stopped. As Helen was set on her feet, a patch of blue appeared over our shoulders in the direction of Conway. True, the sliver of blue was way inland, but the storm appeared to be moving out to sea.

Hands loosened on Helen, and we grinned and shouted, high-fived, and embraced, throwing our arms around the person nearest us. For me that turned out to be Sarge; for Chad, as you would expect, it was Vicki Hester.

Out of each other's embrace, we found ourselves shivering. It had to be a drop in blood sugar.

With the look of one pleased witch, Helen announced, "I do believe this calls for cakes and ale."

Well, it certainly called for something. Perhaps State Farm would ask Helen to come aboard.

With Chad and Sarge assisting Helen back to the house—she seemed exhausted from being possessed by Diana—we returned to the table where Jeremy had cakes and ale along with the horn, seashell, and candle.

Helen blessed the cakes and ale, which had been baked into crescents, and Jeremy passed them around. Helen walked the circle, offering everyone a sip of ale from a cobalt blue goblet.

"Let us eat of the fruits of the earth that we may be reminded of our connection to the gods and goddesses of our world. Let us drink of the fruits of the earth that we may be renewed and refreshed as we partake of the earth's gifts. Blessed be."

With a finger at his lips, Jeremy cautioned us to remain silent. He didn't have to. We fell on the meager food with the heartiest of appetites.

Once fortified, Lady Light released the elements associated with the four points of the compass in reverse order. That done, she thanked us for our single-mindedness of purpose in turning back the hurricane.

The words were no more out of Helen's mouth when Vicki Hester began to shake and tremble and collapsed to the floor.

Chapter 5

arge got to her first. I think the rest of us were in a daze. It wasn't something you expected when you came out of a trance. Of course, I'm not sure what to expect coming out of a trance.

Sarge snapped off his belt, pried open the girl's mouth, and slid the belt between her teeth as Vicki's head bobbed and her arms twitched. I shook my head, trying to remove the cobwebs. Our group was back in the real world—the one with the hurricane.

Oh, yeah. The hurricane was gone.

Yeah. Right. Had anyone looked outside lately?

Still, I heard no sounds from outside, perhaps some light rain on the metal roof of the porch, but that could've been my imagination.

By the glow of the light from the candles in the living room and the single one on the altar, my fiancé joined Sarge. The two men bent over the well-endowed woman.

"What's wrong with her?" Chad asked the former sergeant.

"The energy from the circle was probably too much for her." When we all looked at Helen, she explained,

"She is, after all, just a beginner at the craft."

We returned our attention to the woman on the floor. She was doing some version of the Saint Vitus' dance: shoulders rising and falling, fingers grasping for things that weren't there, and arms and legs doing the herky-jerky.

Sarge slapped Vicki's face.

Chad jerked back. "What'd you do that for?"

Vicki's eyes popped open and she looked at Sarge. "Why'd you do that?" She touched her face.

"You left us for the spirit world."

"She wasn't in the spirit world," said our witch. "You're not listening to me, Mr. Jackson"—I'd forgotten Sarge's surname—"as when I told you not to remain here once you'd checked the security." Helen gestured at us. "I will not have anyone here who is not in tune with the craft."

At this remark my fiancé looked at me.

"Everyone back," ordered Sarge. "Give her room to breathe."

Chad sat upright, hands resting on his knees, and we all stepped back, but not too far. Perhaps we wanted to remain within the safety of the circle.

I glanced over my shoulder. No warm glow surrounding us now. Only Brandon Calhoun with his mouth hanging open and Reynolds Pearce chewing on his lip.

"What happened, Vicki?" asked Chad.

The Hester girl shook her head, then asked. "I don't know . . ." She looked from Sarge to Chad. "Could you help me sit up?"

"Are you sure you're okay?" asked my fiancé.

Vicki nodded, and the two men gave her a hand.

"What did you feel?" asked Jeremy, once Vicki was upright.

"Everything began to get dimmer." She looked at the

table. "I thought the candle was going out, but—"

"Did you feel anything inside of you?"

"Jeremy, please . . ." said Lady Light.

If Jeremy Knapp was here to collect experiences, then he was certainly having the time of his life. And encouraging the girl, it would appear.

"I don't remember." Vicki glanced at the stub of a candle burning on the table/altar. "I remember the light dimming; them something stung my face." She looked at the former sergeant, who held her arm.

"This whole experience might have been too much for her," suggested Chad. "Maybe she needs to—"

"No, no," said Vicki, glancing at Jeremy before shaking off Sarge's hand. "I'm okay. Help me to my feet."

"Maybe if she took a seat in the living room," I suggested. But if she made a beeline for the sofa, I would, too, even if I had to fight my fiancé for the right to hold this girl's hand.

Now standing, and with that little-girl smile of hers, Vicki said, "If it's all the same to everyone, I wouldn't mind something to eat."

"There are the cakes and ale to be finished," said Helen, gesturing at the table. "And dry clothing to get into before dinner."

Sarge accompanied our small troop up the winding staircase to the upstairs bedrooms. Chad's and mine held two single beds and was at the rear of the second floor. Sarge did not appear to occupy one of the five bedrooms but slept on a cot at the top of the stairs. On the cot lay a duffle bag.

Our room had a single shuttered window, but by now we were used to candles and flashlights. Chad had brought along a light that converted from a large flashlight into a lantern-like device. He sat it on the nightstand between our twin beds, breaking the spell of darkness. Still no sound of wind or rain from outside.

Pulling off his wet clothing, Chad glanced from one narrow bed to the other. "Are we both going to be able to fit into one of those?"

If he was smiling, I didn't see it. After swinging my pack from my shoulder, I had collapsed on the bed, wet clothes and all, shoulders slumped, head bent forward, arms across my knees. A hollowness seemed to have filled me, a huge gaping hole quickly filling with despair. It was that same feeling I had when Chad did not sleep over, and I was left alone on an old fishing boat moored at Wacca Wache Landing.

Tears ran down my cheeks as I watched Chad dry himself with a towel taken from his pack and then pulled on a pair of ripcord pants and a short-sleeved shirt. He brushed back his wet brown hair after glancing in a mirror over the dresser. Returning to the other bed to put on a pair of dry running shoes, he found me lying on my bed, arm across my eyes.

"Don't you think you should get out of those wet clothes?" he asked.

I couldn't reply.

"Suze, are you all right?"

"Just . . . a little . . . tired."

From the hallway, Sarge announced that everyone was meeting in the kitchen for dinner. I don't know where Sarge had cleaned up. Perhaps in the dysfunctional bathroom across the hall.

"Why don't you stay here and rest," encouraged Chad. "I'm sure supper's not ready yet."

"No," I said, using my arm to brush my tears away, "I'm ready."

I sat up quickly and bent over to pull off a wet

running shoe—and found Chad on his knees in front of me, like the night he proposed in the moonlight at the Landing. He raised my chin and looked at my face. Turning aside, I wiped away more tears.

"Ceremony get to you?" he asked.

"I don't know. Something got to me."

Chad helped me remove my shoes and wet socks, and when the waterworks wouldn't stop, he sat beside me on the bed and put his arms around me.

"Chad . . ."

"Yes?"

"I don't think . . ."

He held me tight, and I leaned into his shoulder. Still, the tears didn't stop.

"Suze, the storm's gone. We can leave, if that's what you want."

"I think . . . it's best *I* leave."

He gripped my shoulders with both hands, turned me on the edge of the bed, and held me where he could see me. "You're not biking out of here without me."

"But I don't belong here," I said, helplessly.

"What do you mean?" His hands were tight on my shoulders now.

I wiped more tears away. "I don't belong here and you know it."

"What BS," he said, taking me into his arms, a safe and warm place to be. "Wherever one of us is, that's where the other one's to be."

Tears continued to run down my face as I looked over his shoulder. I sniffled.

He held me out at arm's length again. "Come on, Suze. The storm's over. Everything's fine."

"Okay," I said, wiping away what I hoped was the last of the tears. "Let me get into some dry things and work on my face."

"Your face always looks excellent to me."

We used the backstairs to reach the ground floor, and through another set of doors leading to the house's main hallway, the same ones I'd seen when I'd first entered the house, I could see there was more to the house than the living room and the room where the ritual had been performed.

Across from the ritual room was a den or study containing comfortable chairs with footrests. Working my flashlight around, I saw walls filled with books and lamps strategically placed for reading. A woven area rug covered the hardwood floor, a grandfather clock stood guard near the door, and kindling and chunks of dry wood had been laid on the hearth for the first winter's chill. On the mantelpiece were pictures of various families enjoying their stay at the beach. There were even more on the walls of the room.

Adjoining this study was the formal dining room and an adjoining door. In it a long oak table was set for dinner, gleaming with silverware, colorful tablemats, and a centerpiece arrangement of freshly cut flowers. Six high-backed red satin chairs sat around the table. Two more chairs at each end made it possible to seat eight.

Hmm. If the redhead had remained behind, where would I have sat?

The remaining furnishings were similar to the table, with red satin curtains at shuttered windows at the far end of the room. A chandelier hung over the table, though no light radiated from its bulbs. Along the Grand Strand, smart people had even turned off their gas and water.

"Pretty impressive." Chad's beam of light had stopped on the sideboard.

Above a silver service hung a portrait. The father stood behind the chair where his wife sat. Flanking the mother were two girls, and sitting in her lap, a small boy. All were dressed formally and from the turn of the century. Both girls wore frilly dresses, the boy a sailor suit.

Crossing the dining room to the sideboard, I used a door that exited from the other side. I found myself in an anteroom leading to a half bath on my right, and across the hallway, the kitchen.

Gesturing toward the kitchen, I asked, "You're not afraid that Vicki Hester won't need your assistance again?"

Chad joined me in the small room. "Oh, I don't think . . . Suze, you can't possibly believe—"

I faced him, determined not to cry. I would not use that weapon. Yet. "It doesn't really matter what I think, does it?" I felt my chin rise and my jaw clench. For the first time I realized Chad's unruly brown hair hung over his forehead and I didn't have the least interest in brushing it back in place. Another thing of which I was certain: I was in Chad's world now, and, once again, I didn't like what I was seeing. Or feeling, hence the waterworks upstairs.

"Come on, Suze, we were ride buddies in high school. We didn't even date."

I crossed my arms across my tee, certainly not white in this weather. "Actually, I'm more concerned why we're really here. Specifically why you're here."

Chad glanced at the spacious kitchen. It appeared the men were pitching in. Since I wasn't much of a cook, that would be my kind of a kitchen. I, however, had domestic work of my own.

"Chad, we are not going to begin our marriage this way, and if you haven't noticed, that's only a couple of months away."

"Two months, six days."

"You're . . . you're counting?" I felt my mouth remain open longer than necessary to utter those words.

Chad was grinning. "You're not the only one who wants to get married."

Though that was music to my ears and my arms unfolded from my chest, I wouldn't be sidetracked. "Chad, why are you here?"

"To participate in a hurricane party." He glanced toward the front of the house. "Now I'll have to wait for the next one."

Not if I have anything to do with it. "There's been something weird about this from the get-go and I want you to come clean. Or the wedding's off."

"You've got to be kidding." Now his smile was gone.

I refolded my arms across my chest. Yes, yes, I know, where he could see the ring—if the damn diamond would remind him of anything. "I want to know why these people have gathered in this house."

"We all knew each other in school, that's all."

"And you, a person who can remember having few friends from high school; Helen McCuen just happened to invite you to her hurricane party."

"I thought you knew Helen."

"Not like you do."

"Oh, don't start that again."

"I didn't mean it the way you took it."

He breathed deeply and let it out. "If you know anything about Helen, she's always playing to the crowd."

"You're saying you don't know jack about what's going on in this house?"

"Susan, believe me, there's nothing going on."

"Then you won't mind if I ask a few questions."

Chad smiled. "I wouldn't have it any other way."

The kitchen was laid out as follows: To my right was a door to a walk-in pantry, to the left a small alcove. That's where Sarge sat on a chair drinking a Coors, and where I saw the first phone I'd seen in the house. It was mounted on the wall. Not that it would work. Sarge was watching a small battery-powered black-and-white TV on a counter alongside a phone book, notepad, and writing instruments. The flickering signal came from WBT in Charlotte. Sarge was monitoring the position of the hurricane on his notepad.

"Looks like she's moving out to sea." After another swig from his beer, he added, "But I wouldn't be planning on leaving. It'll be dark soon, and if that hurricane decides to . . ."

A withering glare from Helen McCuen silenced him.

"I'm just saying we should play it safe, ma'am."

"I know what you were saying, Mr. Jackson," said Helen with ice hanging from every word.

In front of the TV lay Sarge's cell phone, usually worn on his hip, and the Phillips screwdriver I thought Jeremy Knapp had used to shutter the back door. Straight across the kitchen was a double sink with modern, stainless steel fixtures under shuttered windows. On one side of the double sink sat a huge metal container where you could twist a black knob at its bottom and fill your water bottle. In the sink was a cooler filled with ice, and sticking their heads out of the ice, bottles of water. To the right of that, a large camp stove sat on a piece of plywood covering the surface of a modern gas range, and a huge pot of soup sat on both burners. Jeremy Knapp was holding the top of the metal pot with a potholder mitt and peering inside.

Holding up the stirring spoon, Jeremy smiled at us.

"Tastes pretty good for a bunch of vegetables."

The spoon held bits of colorful ingredients, along with a rather large, pale green bay leaf. He returned the spoon to the pot and continued to stir. Reynolds Pearce hovered nearby as if looking for something to do.

Helen McCuen had opened a Tupperware container that held corn muffins. "That's high praise coming from someone who usually elbows people away from the stove, Jeremy."

Next to the range was a double-door refrigerator on which sat the munchies Vicki Hester had brought into the house. A large camp lantern sat among the plastic bags, and I wondered if anyone knew how combustible potato chips could be.

Brandon Calhoun, our LARP, sat in the middle of the room at a long, wide island with another lantern. He was breaking up lettuce as Vicki Hester sliced tomatoes. Both sat on barstools. Hester appeared to have recovered from her episode in the ritual room. Color had returned to her face, her damp brown hair was pulled back into a ponytail, and she had another smile for my fiancé. Brandon Calhoun appeared rather glum as he broke up the lettuce with his bony white fingers. The pieces of lettuce would, I hoped, be rinsed with water from the large metal container sitting to one side of the double sink.

"Is there something we can do?" asked Chad.

I was checking the walk-in pantry. Fiancé or not, I was not completely comfortable around these people.

"Almost done," said Helen as she placed the muffins on a plate. "I started the soup before we formed the circle. It should be ready by now."

As if on cue, Vicki scooped up a strainer containing the sliced tomatoes, cucumbers, and pieces of lettuce, and trotted over to double sink where she rinsed the lettuce for the salad under the spigot on the large water can. Thank you, Vicki.

Seeing Reynolds Pearce idle, Helen said, "Chad, if you'll take the cheese from the cooler, Reynolds can grate it for the salad. Reynolds, the grater's under the counter to the left of the sink."

Chad did and Reynolds began working on the cheese at the island.

"I brought croutons," Vicki said from the sink. "They're on the fridge."

"Let's stick with what's natural, why don't we?"

"Croutons are made from bread. What's the problem?"

"Vicki, since you are a guest in my home I would appreciate that the dinner go as planned." Helen glanced at the refrigerator where the colorful sacks of junk food sat. "Besides, your croutons are more than toasted bread."

A belch from Sarge drew our attention to his alcove-corner of the room. "I'm starving myself." He stood and rubbed his stomach that, since he wore no foul-weather gear, revealed a bit of a paunch and a pretty good set of forearms. "I'll eat anything."

"Bowls are in the cupboard on the far side of the sink, Mr. Jackson," said Helen, gesturing to where Vicki was now dumping equal portions of lettuce, tomato, and cucumbers into white salad bowls.

At the preparation island, Reynolds stopped grating the cheese. "I don't eat cucumbers." Reynolds saw us staring at him. "Disagrees with me."

"Probably it's your job," commented Jeremy from where he was turning off the gas under the pot of soup.

"Now, now," said Helen, "no shop talk."

Sarge took down the soup bowls and Vicki suggested

that Reynolds toss his cucumbers into the sink. Then she took the board with the grated cheese to the other side of the sink and began sprinkling cheese on the salads. From the corner, Brandon Calhoun, resplendent in black, observed but said nothing.

"Chad, the dressing is in the cooler. Made it myself," Helen added proudly.

My fiancé took the bottle from the cooler and placed it on the counter near the sink. Vicki tried to engage Chad in conversation, but Chad asked if he could fix me a salad. He fixed two, then carried them into the dining room.

Which is where we soon found ourselves, and the answers to some of my questions. Which led to even more questions.

Sarge moved in after we were all seated, pouring iced tea or bottled water. Helen sat at the far end of the table, Jeremy at the opposite end, a long line of candles in brass holders separating them. Across from Chad sat Vicki Hester, where he couldn't miss her smile. Flanking the little twit were the anxious Reynolds Pearce and the silent Brandon Calhoun. Actually, I was beginning to think Brandon Calhoun was out of his league. Our investment banker, I was soon to learn, didn't have any doubt.

Sarge sat on the other side of Chad near Jeremy at the far end of the table. Corn muffins were passed around, and butter came out for those who wanted it. We all dug in to soup in oversized bowls fired in someone's kiln. No bowl had the same shape or color, and all were earth tones. From what I could tell, the soup contained onions, carrots, celery, garlic, tomatoes, potatoes, turnips, butter beans, and corn. Seasoning came from salt, pepper, and thyme.

Hunger decimated conversation until Jeremy said, "Well, Reynolds, I guess you believe in witchcraft now."

"Oh," said Vicki, grinning at the investment banker sitting beside her, "with what Lady Light did to his business, I imagine he was a believer long before he came to Myrtle Beach."

The investment banker only stared into his soup.

"Reynolds," said Helen, "I said I would see what I could do for you and I certainly will."

Reynolds did not look up from his bowl.

Lady Light looked to the far end of the table. "Jeremy, I guess you wonder why I haven't cursed you?"

"The thought had crossed my mind."

"Who says I haven't?"

Spoon almost at his mouth, Jeremy stuttered, "What—what do you mean?"

"Who's to say all this globetrotting you do isn't something I wished on you—so you'd become more familiar with Mother's bountiful world after leading such a shallow existence. You've seen more of Mother's world than anyone at this table, haven't you?"

Our collector of experiences put down his spoon. "That's bending the facts to suit you."

"As long as she's not bending spoons," I said. "I plan on having more of that delicious soup."

Sarge was immediately through the door and returning with the pot. Hmmm. Protecting me not withstanding, it's always good for every busy woman to have a wife.

Sarge held the pot with two potholders and leaned down so I could ladle more soup into my bowl. He moved around the table allowing others to refill their bowls. Most did. Evidently cakes and ale had not been enough. Nor that first bowl of soup.

After a few more spoonfuls of what could only be described as some of the best vegetable soup I'd ever eaten, I said, "All of you have good reason to be here."

When heads turned in my direction, I added, "Other than the hurricane party, which, for most people would be quite enough."

"I'm studying the craft," Vicki volunteered from the other side of the table.

I remembered Vicki from The Attic when she had to be the center of attention. The way she did that was by mastering every new dance that came along. Since I was a few years younger, Vicki intrigued me, until I saw how she played one boy against another, and joked about it in the rest room.

"So there's no curse on you?" I asked.

Vicki glanced at the wiccan at the end of the table. To tell the truth, Helen wasn't looking so good, and she hadn't finished her second helping. Her spoon lay beside her bowl, and her face appeared paler than before dinner when she had flitted around the kitchen giving instructions. Oh, well, sooner or later, you had to come down from any high.

Vicki watched Helen's reaction as she responded to my question. "I don't think there's a curse on me. Why would there be?"

I looked down the table. "Sarge overstepped his bounds by remaining behind."

"It's only right," said the pock-faced man returning to his seat. His napkin was stuck in the neck of his shirt. "Things could have gotten out of hand."

"Mr. Jackson . . ." Helen said, "I had things under control. If someone had given off bad vibrations . . . he or she would've been asked . . . to leave. I cannot work—"

"Around bad vibrations," I said, interrupting Helen's faltering voice.

Helen drew in a breath, leaned back in her chair, and studied me. When she spoke again, she appeared to have regained her bearings. "I didn't sense any hostility from you, Susan."

"Or you would've turned me out into the storm."

Helen nodded.

"That wasn't going to happen," said my fiancé.

I couldn't help but flare up. I'm always quick to take offense at the least bit of gallantry. Yes, yes, I know I've got some work to do in that area. "Because you were here, Chad?"

"Mr. Jackson would've turned Susan away."

"That's nuts," said my protector. "There was a storm outside."

Helen smiled. "And now there is no storm."

"Because she turned it away," finished Vicki, beaming. "I'm hoping she'll show me her tricks."

"There are no tricks," said Helen, "only harmony."

"That's not the point," Chad said, looking from Sarge sitting behind him to Helen at the far end of the table. "You don't send people out into a storm."

"Mr. Jackson would have made sure Susan reached safety."

"That would have been a trick," I offered.

"I have a vehicle," said Sarge. "That's why I was chosen for this job."

"A vehicle that can stand up to a hurricane." I said that, but everyone turned and stared at the former army sergeant.

"An APC."

"A what?" asked Vicki.

"Armored personnel carrier," Sarge explained to the girl across the table.

"Yeah. Right."

"Miss Chase, my vehicle is street legal. I have the proper papers and a tag. It's parked farther inland."

Helen confirmed this. "I wasn't going to have some military vehicle near the ceremony."

Driving away from a hurricane in an APC was beyond belief, so I looked at our LARP. "Brandon, are you going to tell us why you're here?"

The long-nosed, pale young man cleared his throat. "To play out the greatest drama in life."

"Well, you'd better get on with it. All I've seen is you standing around with your mouth hanging open."

The phone in my jeans sounded the theme from *Hawaii 5-0*. "Yes?" I asked into a flip-top phone pulled from a pocket. The cell phone was with me, along with my Lady Smith & Wesson upstairs in my pack, for what might happen *after* the hurricane.

"Hey, babe, that you?" came a high-pitched male voice over the phone.

"Who's this?"

"Who you think, babe?"

"Kenny?" Meaning Kenny Mashburn, drug dealer and local sleazeball. "How did you get this number?"

Everyone was staring at me. I was hunched over, away from Chad, leaning toward Helen. Lady Light raised an eyebrow. I ignored her.

"Babe, remember how you said you could trap my phone and trip me up good?"

I didn't know what to say to that so I said nothing.

"I done it to you."

"To what advantage?" I asked.

"You're hanging at a hurricane party?"

"You've got that wrong. I'm inland."

"Right," said Kenny with a laugh. "Susan Chase afraid of a little ol' hurricane. Got any white girls there?

Oughta be really pumped thinking that 'cane gonna blow them out to sea."

Looking across the table at an excited Vicki Hester, I said, "There's just me."

"Susan Chase the only gal at a party sure to get the juices flowing. I'll be right over."

"The hurricane's gone," I said, the only defense I could think of. "The witch you saw on TV drove it away." I glanced at Helen, who was giving me the evil eye.

"She's not the only one," said Kenny with a laugh. "I spent the last couple of hours with some crazy guy cutting up chickens and talking to the bird's innards. He's called CNN and already taking credit for Lili turning tail and running. Listen, back to the babes—"

I closed the phone, and when I sat up, I saw everyone staring at me. "Get the door. It's Domino's."

Everyone laughed, though some nervously. Anyone with any sense had left the Grand Strand days ago. I remember Lt. J.D. Warden chiding me.

"You're going to do what?"

In New York, J.D. had taken a bullet in the line of duty, then moved south, and spent a few years working for SLED. Now, he now lives on disability, plays golf, fishes, and attends to his grandkids. What's so annoying about the guy is he acts like he's my father.

"Chad wants to attend a hurricane party."

"That doesn't explain why you have to be there."

"I'm engaged to the guy, if you don't remember."

"So this Rivers kid turns out to be a bust. Move on."

That really ticked me off. I already had the dress picked out, the date set, and a ring on my finger. Once, several months back, when Mr. Rivers, Senior, had smiled and asked if his son was treating me right, I held out my hand. "You don't see a ring there, do you?"

Mr. Rivers swallowed hard, his wife's hand came up to her throat as she gasped, and Chad said, "Suze, I really don't think—"

I turned on him, eyes ice-cold. "Well, your father asked."

It wasn't long before I had a ring on my finger and a date set, in case Dr. Laura was asking.

"Susan," said Helen, "I asked that no cell phones be brought into this house." She extended a hand. There was no ring on that hand either.

I gave up the phone, which, it would appear, caused it to sound off again. Helen tried to ignore it, but the phone continued to play the theme from *Hawaii 5-O*. Finally, she opened the cell, listened, and said, "We don't need assistance. Of course, if you want to stop by." She gave our address.

"The Horry County Police Department," explained Helen to everyone when she closed the phone. "They appear to want to meddle."

"But why would they call you on my cell?" I asked.

Chapter 6

Whice others did the dishes, Helen took me by the arm and ushered me down the hall and back to the living room. I took a seat on the red velvet sofa as she towered over me in her dark dress with its long sleeves. The quarter moons sparkled when light from one of the candles hit her silver earrings. Still, the room lacked the intimacy it had once held, though the chairs were still in place, the double doors to the ritual room closed, and Sarge had installed a set of fresh candles. The incense bowl appeared to have been allowed to burn out and there was no longer the sound of that piano being played in minor chords, wherever that had come from. Possibly a hidden boom box looped to play forever.

"It's appropriate you should be here, Susan."

"And why is that?"

"Another Doubting Thomas brought to heel."

"Helen, I wouldn't get up on your high horse just yet. Lili is one of the most erratic hurricanes of the season. She could return at any time."

"She won't." Jerking a thumb in the direction of

the rear of the house, she added, "None of those fools believed I could do it. All I asked for was an open mind. And they gave it to me, hoping I'd fail. You even played along."

"Well, there was my own ass to consider." I leaned back against the sofa. "Would you've really sent me out into the storm?"

"Of course not," she said, taking a seat beside me. "I would've lost your fiancé."

"What's the connection there?"

She smiled slyly. "He hasn't told you." After settling into the other end of the couch, she asked, "Susan, who's to say I didn't bring the two of you together."

"Helen, you're full of it. I met Chad at the beach, like I do a good many other guys."

"Perhaps I was the one who sent him your way."

I shook my head. "Monday morning quarterbacking, like telling Jeremy you had sent him on a quest around the world."

"But you must agree it has become a rather interesting experiment."

"In what?" Taunting never brought out the best in me. Under every little taunt, there's an element of truth.

"That someone such as Chad Rivers could possibly fall for a street person? Come on, Susan, we both know Chad's about as perfect as they come. Why would he take an interest in you?"

"To walk on the wild side?" I said, playing along.

"For two years? What could possibly hold his attention? You have no family, come from the wrong side of the tracks, and what you call home is a dilapidated shrimp boat left to you when your father got drunk, fell overboard, and drowned. You have little education, you're unsophisticated"—she looked me over—"and you don't even know how to dress. What other explanation could there be?"

I shrugged. "Shit happens."

Helen didn't care for that answer, so I gave her another one. "Okay, Helen, you're hot stuff and everything has happened as you've said, but why is Chad here? What did you have to prove to him?"

"He lives at the beach. Builds boats. Next time he's running for shelter from an approaching storm, he'll wish he had me onboard." She sat up, slapping her knees. "So all of you will leave this house bearing the mark of the craft."

"Gosh, Helen, but that makes you the center of the universe for a good number of people."

"And more in the future. You think I didn't turn back the hurricane, so be it. You want to think I didn't bring you and Chad together for my own amusement, think what you may." She gestured toward the rear of the house. "If Jeremy wants to think he has a mind of his own, what do I care? I know better."

"And Brandon Calhoun. What possible reason could you have for inviting him here? Why would you have to prove anything to him?"

Helen tossed her long blond hair. "Brandon tried to become a witch but didn't have the talent or the dedication. He had to settle for role-playing and futzing around with graphic comic books. He's a wannabe, like Vicki Hester." She paused. "And there's the fact that a smaller circle wouldn't have worked."

"Then it goes without saying that Reynolds Pearce believes you put a curse on his investment firm—which raises the point that if you're powerful enough to turn away a hurricane, why would it be so difficult to turn a few heads on any Fortune 500 company."

"I wasn't at the height of my powers then."

"Yeah. Right."

"You don't believe me?"

"Helen, I don't believe much of anything, but I was curious about how you got a mouse like Reynolds Pearce to risk his life by attending a hurricane party."

She shrugged. "I simply walked around his home office several hours a day for a week."

"And their investments began to go south? All of them?"

She nodded. "Most of them. It was in all the Charlotte paper, on TV. I was interviewed on *John Boy & Billy*—some witch had put a curse on an investment firm in Charlotte."

"So he's come to pay homage to the great Lady Light."

"As all should do. As more will."

She stared at the windows as if she were looking much farther away than their shutters. Inside the house was quiet as a tomb. Or a wiccan's circle.

Without looking at me, she explained. "No one on his board listened when Reynolds proposed the expansion of my web site through a massive publicity campaign. Server costs are negligible, including the DSL hookup. I could finance those through contributions."

She returned her attention to me. "There are over a billion web pages. How do you break through that sort of clutter without a massive publicity campaign?"

"After this stunt with the hurricane—if they have celebrity boxing, why not witchcraft?"

Her frustration got her on her feet. She strode across the room, standing with her back to me and at the entrance to the hallway. "The networks are controlled by Christians, or those afraid of offending them. Cable, however, is hungry for infomercials, and while I'll be lumped with psychics, weight-loss products, and get-rich-quick schemes, it'll give me the platform to introduce people to the craft, and finally to build the first worldwide coven. A worldwide coven is something witchcraft has needed for centuries. There are too many splinter groups."

"And you're the one to unite them."

"It's my destiny."

"Since you've brought up the possibility of a worldwide church of witches—"

"Coven."

"Whatever. Where'd you go to church, Helen?"

Startled, she faced me. "What?"

"Where'd you go to church?"

She shrugged. "We didn't."

"Are you aware that most witches come from families poorly grounded in faith. It doesn't matter what religion—"

"I don't care for amateur shrinks."

"Or professional ones, it would appear."

She returned to the sofa and towered over me. "Now what does that mean?"

"You stopped going to your shrink."

"And how would you know that?"

"We shared the same shrink . . . a few years back." I shrugged. "A friend of mine thought it might help me deal with my hostility."

"My therapy accomplished nothing."

"Yeah, yeah. The shrink was probably asking why you had to test the limits of parental love. Your parents trusted you, believed you were something special, and what did that get them? A witch."

"And your parents—"

"Did nothing."

"Oh, the little you've accomplished you did on your own." She smiled down at me. "Maybe you had help you don't even know about."

"I doubt it. All I accomplished happened before you were at the height of your powers."

She glared at me, and then she had another of those little turns that appeared to weaken her resolve. Her face went pale and her eyes lost their focus.

"Helen, are you all right?" I reached for her.

Ignoring my hand, she sat at the other end of the couch. "Probably . . . too much rush from repelling the storm."

"At least you've won over Vicki Hester."

"She's . . . she's under the thumb of Jeremy. She'll do anything he says."

That's not the way I remembered. All Vicki Hester's attention had been focused on my fiancé, and I damn well remembered that!

Jeez. I was getting jealous in my old age.

Well, at least I wasn't alone with those thoughts. Chad stood at the door.

"Susan?"

"Yes," I said, standing and moving in his direction.

"I was wondering if you could help me check the roof."

"The roof?" asked Helen, not rising. "What's wrong with the roof?"

"Probably nothing, but I've lived at the beach long enough that I want to make sure everything's secure."

"Didn't you see me . . . drive away the hurricane?"

"Helen, I'm not impugning you're ability. I simply want to check the roof and I want someone to go along." He headed down the hall. "Or she can stay here and make girl talk with you."

"It's not . . . girl talk," was the last thing I heard from Helen as I joined my fiancé in the hallway.

"What's the problem?" I asked, following him.

Chad said nothing until we reached the narrow pair of doors leading to the rear of the house. On the other side of the doors was the staircase that climbed the kitchen wall—and to our rooms. Gee, I wouldn't mind a quick stop there on the way to the roof. You know the saying: Nothing loosens a bra strap like a good scare.

I could hear voices from the kitchen, chattering about the latest position of the hurricane. Lili had stalled once again, as if trying to make up her mind which way to go.

Chad lowered his voice to say, "I don't want you talking to Helen."

"And why's that?"

"You know, Suze, sometimes you're going to have to accept the fact that your future husband might know what's best for you."

"Chad, I don't think—"

"I'm getting a little tired of listening to what Susan Chase thinks. Did you ever think others may have had enough, too?"

"Chad, I don't think—"

"There you go again. Thinking."

I felt my hands go to my hips. All thoughts of a quickie vanished from my mind. "I'm not taking this from you."

He glanced in the direction of the kitchen. "Lower your voice. That's your problem. You don't take crap from anyone. Did you ever think your future husband might have his family's best interests at heart?"

"And maybe that future husband would ask my opinion."

"It might not be a decision a woman's capable of making."

"Chad, I don't think you want to go there."

His eyebrow arched. "So you don't have to consider

the possibility, however remote, that anyone but you can raise our children." He shook his head. "You've been watching too much TV."

"Come again?"

"All husbands on TV are idiots, but, then again, how would you sell anything to women if husbands were portrayed as competent."

"Chad, what are you trying to say?"

"That I want to take care of our family, but most important I want to know that I can occasionally make unilateral decisions in the best interest of our family." He paused as if to collect his thoughts. "You know how my mother loves her soaps?"

I nodded, that being the only response I could think of. Where was this conversation headed?

"And you know they had damn little money when they started out because my grandfather had bankrupted her family before he committed suicide and my father had to work his way through Georgia Tech."

"Yes, but—"

"My mom had to work in the office and didn't get to see her favorite story."

"Honey, what does this have to do with us?"

"My father bought the first VCR and microwave. My mother thought he was being terribly extravagant, but when my father saw what those two appliances might do for the family, he purchased them and brought them home."

I smiled. "So you want the right to buy stuff for me. You've got it."

"Don't trivialize what I'm saying."

"I'm sorry, I'm sorry. Truly, I'm just trying to understand."

"Try thinking about yourself less." He took me into his arms and inclined his head in the direction of the dining room. "You gave me an ultimatum about fessing up about Helen McCuen and now I'm returning the favor."

"I don't think I understand."

I saw Helen staring at us from the living room door. To do this she had to hold onto the jamb. Her face was still deathly pale.

Raising my voice over the sound of wind that appeared to be rising again, I asked, "Helen, are you all right?"

"Yes . . . yes."

"Go sit back down until you get your wheels under you." To Chad, I said, "Maybe I should go sit with her."

"I don't want you around that woman."

I pushed him away. "What is it between you two? I took your word about the Hester girl because I wanted to believe there wasn't anything—"

"If there had been, it would've been none of your business."

"Granted, but you were invited here by Helen, not Vicki."

Chad considered this, then left me, crossed the hall and entered the study. I followed him. Standing in the middle of the woven carpet and surrounded by shelves of books, he was silent for a long time. Behind me, the grandfather clock ticked away. The wind appeared to be trying to break into the house from the north. That was odd. Hurricane winds came from the direction of the storm, not to mention that the storm was supposed to be gone.

"It's not something I want to tell you because you'll laugh. No. You'll be amused," he said with a slight smile that was on his face when he turned around. "The street-savvy Susan Chase would be very amused at the . . . thing between Helen McCuen and me."

Well, sometimes you have to let them get around to it in their own special way.

"Helen dared me to show and I did." He stared into the unlit fireplace, then shook his head. "Sometimes I wonder about the women I'm attracted to."

"So you were an item. In a past life."

"We dated in high school," he said without emotion.

"I get the impression more than one person in this house attended Conway High School."

"All of us did."

I tried to comprehend this—because that would include Sarge, but I was more interested in the hold Helen McCuen held over my fiancé. "So she called you?"

"She didn't have to. What she was doing was in the paper and everywhere on TV."

"So it was a dare left over from high school, like climbing a water tower, and you failed to reach Helen's expectations."

There was a long sigh before he said, "When we were in high school Helen wanted to have sex. I didn't. Maybe I was scared. Who knows. Not everyone's like those kids on *Dawson's Creek.*"

I waited for him to continue. "That's it?"

"That's it."

"So to prove what a man you are you came to a hurricane party." I shook my head. "Men."

He closed with me. "Hey, it's not like you haven't been trying to prove you're the equal of any guy."

I didn't know what to say to that.

"And when you accuse me of having relations with two different women within a matter of hours, it makes me wonder what I'm getting myself into."

Chad looked beyond me toward the rear of the house. "You haven't asked me one single question about the men, but for the record, I didn't want anything to do with these people, but my mother insisted. I tried to tell her that no matter how popular Jeremy and Helen were, they weren't the right kind of friends. Besides, I didn't want friends. I had my designs."

The first time Chad told me he had his designs, we'd been lounging against a very large piece of driftwood in front of a fire on a beach well away from the lights of Myrtle Beach. And to get away from the lights along the Grand Strand, you really had to go a ways. Anyway, when my main man said he "had his designs," I replied, "And your father's influence and money."

Chad shook his head. "My dad doesn't have what it takes to design boats. Ask him and see what he says."

I did and learned the Rivers family considered Chad a prodigy. No one on either side of the family had any talent. My chest swelled with pride as Mr. Rivers said he could only ape what the market wanted, but Chad was the real visionary.

Gee. And I thought I'd fallen for a good-looking guy who happened to have money. Instead, my main man was the future of Rivers Watercrafts, and when he threatened to run off with me and get married, everyone suddenly decided this former lifeguard and runaway finder wasn't such a bad catch.

On that beach a long time ago, I had screwed up the courage to ask, "Chad, why me?"

"I don't know. I just know you're the one for me."

"Come on, honey, if you're messed up because of something your mother did I should—"

"My mother did nothing!" It came out as a shout.

I backed away. Here I was on this remote beach and a long way from home—and probing a raw spot on my boyfriend's psyche.

Chad must've seen something in my eyes. "Hon, I didn't mean that the way it came out. It's just that you're always on my mother's case."

He reached for me, but I scooted away. Rule number one for girls: Never discuss anything important in your lover's arms. Unless it's love, and I'm not even sure about that.

"We don't need them," he said, lowering his arms. "You and I have each other."

I cleared my throat. "I want them."

"But you think my mom's a bitch."

"She's family. She's going to be my family."

He studied me. "That's important to you, isn't it?"

I nodded.

Chad grinned. "Ain't life something. You hate my mother, but you want to be a part of her life."

"Part of her family," I corrected.

"Suze, do you think this is going to work?"

"Are you planning on knocking me up after we're married?"

"Actually, I thought we'd . . . you want babies right away?"

I scooted over to sit beside him. "I may have to spend Sunday brunch with your mom while you're golfing with your dad, but the rest of the week you're all mine."

"And it doesn't concern you that my folks might intrude in our lives?"

With a playful smile, I asked, "Are you planning on inviting them over?"

"No way!"

"Then how can they intrude?"

"My mom might drop by."

"If she does, I won't be wearing a bra, or better yet, something from Victoria Secret you picked out—just for us!"

"That ought to get her," he said, grinning. "Maybe I'll be wearing boxers."

And he took me in his arms and tried to knock me up. However, that wasn't the time or place. I don't trust The Pill or condoms and I make him stay away from me five days of each cycle. The rest of the time we're like rabbits.

Chapter 7

I t had been pretty much of a bust as far as hurricane parties went, and I was killing time while Chad came to grips with the fact that he hadn't lived through a hurricane—yet. But when you lived along the coast there would be plenty of chances in the future.

Not if he wanted to be the father of my babies.

One of the front doors was open, and I walked onto the porch, barely glancing into the living room. It appeared Helen McCuen hadn't moved from the red velvet sofa. She sat, staring straight ahead, actually through me. Some variation of the postpartum blues, I would imagine. I wasn't encouraged to speak. My days with Lady Light were behind me. I was moving on to suburbia; Helen, to change the world.

There's a transformation that comes over a gal offered a chance at the brass ring. Or one with a diamond. It grounds you. One day you're thinking no farther than the weekend; then you're considering living happily ever after. You have no time for the trivial, but go looking for a copy of *Bride* magazine or rent *Father of the Bride* to make sure you've got your shit—er, act together. Have to watch the lingo if you're thinking of having babies.

I tried to get Harry Poinsett involved, you know, picking out the wedding dress and all, but he said that's what girlfriends were for. Unfortunately, I had a tendency to gravitate toward the frivolous—gals who want to go out, get picked up, and dance the night away. Maybe even get laid. I was way short of anyone I could call on to pick out the dress or plan any wedding. An orphan whose credentials might include how to fillet a fish, detect dry rot, or play dollar poker, but not do a wedding. I'd attended very few.

I remembered one young woman who'd been the last of four girls in her family to marry. This young lady had chosen a simple wedding—performed in the same church where her three older sisters had regally marched down an aisle adorned with enough flowers to bury six corpses and lit by enough candlelight to illuminate Carlsbad Caverns, not to mention the long line of bridesmaids, groomsmen, and something sounding like the Mormon Tabernacle Choir in the peanut gallery. Though the booze had flowed like wine at the reception and everyone stuffed themselves silly on hors d'oeuvres, all the talk at the country club had been about how the girl's family must've fallen on hard times to have such a low-key affair.

And I was marrying into the Rivers family?

If you don't think that's a big deal, Chad's mother grew up along the Battery in Charleston, you know, where civilization began: where the Ashley and the Cooper rivers come together. I had to put together something fast, and not embarrass Chad and myself.

At least with the country club set.

Or those along the Battery.

I wasn't sure I wanted to marry in the church, nor did I want to do the tourist thing at the Wedding Chapel by the Sea. Of course, we could always have the service at the beach, where the wedding party gathers in that clump of grass between the hotel pool and the sea oats and the signs warning you to stay off the berm. That, however, had been done to death. I mean, like, I was really in love and I wanted to do something really special, but I was firing blanks, and if I didn't come up with something, Chad's mother would be there, tapping her foot and asking me what was the plan.

Orphaned at fifteen, my only plan had been one of survival without taking the easy way out by selling drugs or my body. Okay, okay, maybe selling drugs was the easy way out for a gal who stood taller than most men and has a tendency to be a little hippy. Anyway, I didn't grow up in suburbia and have parents always on my case about what I was going to do with the rest of my life.

Chad's proposal galvanized my thinking. It had been a moonlit night at Wacca Wache Landing, him down on one knee and the diamond flashing in the overhead lights attracting its share of flying insects. Moments later, I stood waving good-bye with my limp hand, then ducked down into Harry's schooner and shouted my good news. By the time Harry had popped the champagne, I was bawling like a kid whose new toy had been broken only seconds after she's woken up Christmas morning.

"What's wrong, Princess?"

"Like . . ." I sniffed. "Like I told you. Chad wants . . . to marry me." My head bobbed up and down and I sloshed champagne on my hand. I licked it away as Harry asked the grown-up questions.

"I thought that's what you wanted."

"Yes . . ." I gulped, unable to swallow more than a sip. "I want it more . . . than anything."

"Then what's the problem?"

"Harry, I don't know what to do."

"What do you mean?" he asked, taking a seat beside me on the loveseat that subbed for a couch on any schooner.

"I don't know how to plan a wedding."

"All you have to do is find a justice of the peace and—"

"You forget who's the mother of the groom."

Harry nodded, thoughtfully. "This can only mean that you've known if Chad popped the question, his mother was out of the picture, regarding the planning of the wedding, that is."

"And I plan to keep it that way!"

He studied the yellow liquid in his glass as he considered my predicament—along with the last hundred dollars I'd borrowed to make the repairs on the bilge pump to keep *Daddy's Girl* afloat.

"Still, you have you, Chad, and the minister—"

"Harry, are you listening to me?" I sloshed more champagne on my hand turning on him. I wiped it off on my jeans and flicked off the spots that landed on the loveseat.

"Susan, give me a chance to finish."

I did by downing what remained of my champagne, carefully placing the glass on the shelf built into the bulkhead and pulling my knees under my chin—the better to feel sorry for myself.

"You've lived along the Grand Strand how long?"

"I don't know," I said with a shrug. "Ten years?"

"You and I are all who remain of those grandfathered into Wacca Wache Landing before it was sold to that fancy corporation next door." Harry meant the expensive homes across the gravel road from where the boats were moored.

Looking over my knees, I asked, "Your point would be?"

"Didn't you bring Lucy Leslie's killer to justice? And doesn't her father own the Captain's Feast?"

"Her uncle. What are you saying—that I put the arm on him to provide the hors d'oeuvres?"

"I'm sure Mr. Leslie would be willing to make special arrangements."

"I don't know that I have the money to cover it."

"Susan, remember that banker's daughter who was constantly running away and you were always bringing her home from Atlanta? You read him the riot act about not showing the least bit of interest, even in his daughter's report card. How many times did she run away after he began appearing at her school functions and attending her basketball games?"

"Not once."

Harry nodded as if he had untied a mental Gordian knot. "If memory serves, he called and thanked you for how close he and his daughter had become. Your banker friend could make a personal loan. Wachovia recently purchased his bank and he pocketed a substantial amount of money from the sale of his stock."

"He paid for my services. More than most."

"But as a man, he would prefer to be off that hook, about thanking you."

"You guys really are screwed up."

Harry smiled. "And you're about to spend the rest of your life with one."

"I plan on breaking him in."

"As does Chad with you."

I pursed my lip. "You don't think it'll work?"

"The best managers don't try to fit square pegs into round holes. They find those people another position. People cannot change, and if they do, there's an enormous emotional toll. Ever tried to stay on a diet?"

"Could we get back to the wedding? Chad's mom wants her chance to gloat."

"I'm sure she didn't use those exact words."

"Of course not, but she wants some kind of party beyond the after-rehearsal party."

"A celebratory party. Just the sort I would have if my son had married below his station."

"Harry, I never thought . . . ."

A smile crossed his tanned and slim face. "Susan Chase can't take the truth. And the way you dish it out—"

"Enough! Enough!" My hands went to my ears, and when I opened my eyes, I saw he was offering more champagne. "Okay. Where do we start?"

"What do you need?"

"There has to be an archway, if the ceremony's not performed in a church."

"You can rent those. Stan Monk who runs the Grand Strand Rent-All has them."

Nodding, I said, "I did some work for him."

"You helped him raise a boat several years back. Stan made a killing reselling that boat."

"He only paid me by the hour."

"Well, there's the arch. The chairs, too. Where were you thinking of having the ceremony?"

I glanced in the direction of The Waterway, listened as the water lapped against the hull of the schooner. "It's so beautiful here. Tourists don't know about The Waterway, but it's become very special to me."

"Chad proposed here."

I nodded.

"And you want to separate the two?"

"Yes, yes, I do."

"What about Brookgreen Gardens?"

I considered that open expanse of uncluttered and unspoiled space to the south of Murrells Inlet, not far from Wacca Wache Landing.

Some geezer had left his plantation to a foundation, which had removed the house and restored the grounds to their former natural state. Of course, the foundation had added a lot of stuff that had once grown in the area but been driven out by rice, cotton, whatever they'd planted back in slavery days. Once the Big House was gone, in came the sculptures, and if you've driven south from Myrtle Beach on Kings Highway, you've seen the two fighting stallions anchoring the gates to Brookgreen Gardens.

"It would be perfect," I said, with a heavenly sigh.

Harry raised his glass in a toast. "Then Brookgreen Gardens it is. And it's good to see you in love again."

"I've always been in love," I said with a sigh. "From the moment I met him."

"I meant seeing you not stressed over the wedding."

"Let's not go that far. I still have to have a dress."

"Plenty of shops to pick from. Outlets even. This is the Grand Strand."

"And a bridesmaid."

"What about Nancy?"

Nancy Noel was the young woman I'd rescued from white slavery. She still danced topless at the Open Blouse on Highway 501. "And a flower girl."

"Doesn't Mickey DeShields have a daughter?"

Mickey Dee was a black cop who dressed to the nines and worked for SLED. His daughter would know how to dress and she could spread the petals. Still, I pressed, "And music."

"What about that all-girl rock band—the three

runaways who never went home. They started at the Bowery, as did Alabama."

"Couldn't play worth a damn when they started."

"Neither could Bono."

I stared at him.

Harry smiled. "A&E did a profile on U-2."

"Sheesh, Harry, you really had to be desperate for something to watch."

"Actually, it's the good works that Bono does around the world that intrigued me. What would be your song?" Dads smiled wickedly. *"The Wind Beneath My Wings?"*

"No way!"

Now a different kind of a smile. *"I Am Woman* by Helen Reddy?"

"That might be pushing it. I'd rather go with *The Rose."*

Since Bette Midler had popularized *The Rose,* Harry was familiar with the lyrics. "Sounds like a Susan Chase song if there ever was one."

✳　　✳　　✳

A stiff breeze was off the ocean and the sky overcast. Up and down the coast, the Grand Strand was lost in a gray mist that vanished in an unusually heavy fog. Visibility was less than a quarter-mile in either direction; as for the ocean, it disappeared several football fields from shore.

Stepping down from the stairs, I could see behind the house and the sky over Conway, and there was absolutely no blue streak, but, in fact, it was nearing dark. A drizzle and breeze from the north caused me to hustle back onto the porch. Where I ran into Brandon Calhoun.

"I expected more," said the long-nosed young man, with his black hat tipped forward so the rain couldn't reach his face.

Inside the house or out, Brandon always had that hat on, the string hanging under his chin, now fastened tight because of the wind.

I wore a baseball cap. Rain dripped off my bill. Brandon gripped the porch railing with both hands and looked out to sea. Waves still crashed onto the jetty, their dark spray smashing into the far side of the berm.

"I should've brought along more people," he said. "Then we could've really acted this thing out."

"Brandon, get a grip. Helen had control of this from the get-go. You had no place except the role assigned to you. It was that way for all of us." I looked out to sea. "Maybe we were caught up in the moment, maybe we wanted something special to happen." Yeah. Like not having your True Love swallowed up by a hurricane.

He faced me, hands releasing the railing. "And maybe I haven't finished playing out my part."

"Whatever," I threw over my shoulder as I entered one of the open front doors and returned to the house.

This time I didn't even glance in the living room, but I did notice Jeremy in the ritual room. He appeared to be examining the items on the altar.

He looked up, startled. "Oh, didn't see you there."

I entered the room. "Still curious as ever, eh?"

Jeremy put down the feather. One of the items that represented the elements. East, west, north, or south, I didn't remember. A new candle burned in a brass holder on the former altar and illuminated just about everything but the corners of the room.

Jeremy glanced toward the closed doors between us and where Helen McCuen sat on the red velvet sofa.

With a smile, he said, "Who knows if that's what I really wanted?"

"Predestined to be cursed, are you?" I couldn't help but smile.

He stepped away from the altar. "I don't believe for a moment what Helen said. What did she say about you?"

"Why would she say anything? I'm along for the ride."

"The impression I got was that you and she have history."

"Helen was a lifeguard before she became a model. I used to run into her along the Strand. I've known every one of you at one time or another. Except Sarge."

Jeremy grinned. "Yeah, Right, but I don't remember Chad as being that good a dancer."

"Well," I said, holding out my hand with the diamond, "sometimes we gals have to overlook the little things to close the deal."

He laughed.

"Ever thought about getting married?"

He shook his head. "Too much of the world to see."

"So Helen did curse your love life?"

"Not at all. Girl in every port, you know the saying."

"You don't stay in one place long enough to have a decent relationship."

This appeared to offend him. "And how would you know?"

"How would you collect your experiences? You have to keep moving. One-night stands, maybe, but if Helen's cursed you, that's all you'll ever have."

"I believe that about as much as you do, Susan."

"Then that would make us about even."

"I wouldn't say so," he said as I left for the kitchen and

went looking for what was left of the bottled water.

On the way, I passed the smiling face of Vicki Hester. Mentally I made a note to check where Chad was. After the storm, he'd go over the house from top to bottom to understand how it had survived. It wasn't a guy thing, but a boat builder's obsession.

Vicki had come down the back stairs. "Would you believe Chad's on the third floor checking the joists, or whatever they're called?"

"I would." Stone-faced, I continued down the hall and into the kitchen.

Think of it as curiosity; think about it as research; make of it whatever you will, but I did want to know why these people had been chosen to attend this party, and my fiancé most of all. I'm not clairvoyant. I'm no seer. I'm more of a feeler, and something didn't feel right, and I didn't mean the turning back of the storm. That had been downright luck.

Sarge was in front of the black-and-white TV, watching the course, or the non-course, of the storm, another Coors in his hand. He gestured toward the cooler near the sink.

"Have a beer, Miss Chase. I don't want to have to take them back with me."

In front of the small TV was Sarge's cell phone, but not the Phillips screwdriver.

Instead of a beer, I asked, "Job over?"

"I believe it was before the storm arrived."

"Unless you had to bodily carry me out of here."

"Now, Miss Chase," said the former military man, straightening up in his chair, "no reason to hold grudges. Nothing came of it, so there's no reason to dwell on the past."

"Or its possibilities. How do you know these people, Perry?"

The question appeared to catch him off guard. He put down his beer. "I don't know what you're talking about."

"Come on, Sarge. Everyone in this house has history with Helen McCuen." I studied the man with the bald head and pock-marked face. "I'm just trying to figure where you fit into all this."

He got to his feet. "I'm just a working stiff who overstayed my welcome, it would appear." He left the room, leaving me wondering if I really wanted to dull my senses with a beer.

With my flashlight, I poked around in the pantry, saw nothing had changed, and left the kitchen looking for Chad. Through the open set of front doors, I saw him and everyone else huddled together on the porch. A single front door remained open.

I stepped to one side and peered down the hallway. Chad appeared to be agitated about something, and Jeremy was lecturing him. Vicki Hester was staring in my direction. I don't think she saw me because when she turned away to hear what Jeremy had to say, that's when I slipped into the ritual room. Now, to reach the front of the house without them seeing me, I would have to open one of the pocket doors.

I did, rolling it soundlessly into the wall, and crossed the room where Helen McCuen sat—the Phillips screwdriver sticking out of her chest.

Chapter 8

Helen lay back, bubbles popping and moisture dribbling from her slack mouth. A patch of vomit spotted her dress between her breasts, hidden by the folds of the dark bodice. Quickly I put two fingers to the side of her throat.

No pulse.

The Phillips—I supposed it was the Phillips screwdriver because it had the same blue plastic handle—was planted to the hilt in Helen's chest, and if I was correct, the instrument had pierced the side of her left breast, just missing her heart.

I lifted her hands by using the ends of her long sleeves of her dress and examined the palms.

No defensive wounds.

Helen had not fought with her attacker. Too shocked at who was killing her, I would imagine. On the other hand, perhaps she had already been dead.

I dropped her hands.

Gripping the dead woman by the hair, I turned Helen's head left and right, trying to determine if—

"Susan," asked Chad from behind me.

I straightened up, keeping myself between the dead

woman and my fiancé.

The remainder of the party trooped through the door, first Sarge, then Jeremy, finally Reynolds, Vicki, and Brandon Calhoun. All were windblown and damp again. Vicki was patting down her hair and standing very close to my fiancé. There was a cheerful look on her face as she beamed up at Chad.

"Er—yes," I heard myself say.

"It's time we were leaving."

I hadn't known anyone was leaving this late in the day, but that's not what I asked. Gesturing toward the door, I asked, "What was the conference about?"

Chad glanced in the same direction, saw the others behind him. "Just a little theatrics by Brandon."

Our vampire-appearing guest frowned. Well, as long as he didn't bare those ugly fangs.

Taking Chad's arm, Vicki asked, "Do you really have to go? We have the house for as long as we want."

"Not as long as you might think," I said, moving so they could all see Helen McCuen, head lying back against the top of the sofa.

Everyone gaped at the screwdriver planted in her chest. Reynolds Pearce looked like someone had hit him, and, as usual, Brandon Calhoun's mouth fell open, revealing those sharpened incisors. Vicki gasped, then swooned.

There's no other way to describe it. The girl simply went wide-eyed, her hand came up to the side of her head, and her eyes rolled back. Soon she was in a heap on the floor behind Chad.

My fiancé didn't see her fall. He was already at the couch, kneeling and leaning into the sofa. "My God, Susan, what happened?"

"Lady Light appears to have been murdered."

On the other side of me, in the light from the

open doorway, Jeremy slid to his knees, gripped the screwdriver, and pulled it out.

"My God!" he shouted. "This wasn't necessary."

Once the screwdriver was removed, the fabric in the wiccan's dark clothing closed as if the screwdriver had never been there. There was no blood on the screwdriver. The brown and white vomit, mixed with the color of some of the soup's vegetables, rolled down her chest and dropped into her lap.

Jeremy gripped the dead woman by the shoulder. He looked at me. "But why?"

"We'll soon know," I said, "but right now you're tampering with a crime scene."

Jeremy looked from Helen to me, then to the screwdriver. He dropped the Phillips into the lap of Lady Light, right in the small heap of vomit.

Sarge shouldered his way past my fiancé, reached down, and put fingers against Helen's throat. He straightened up and nodded. "Dead for sure." Sarge looked at me. "Was it you that done it, Chase?"

"She was dead when I found her."

"Or after you killed her," accused Jeremy.

I stepped back, readying myself as I do when confronted with any jerk. "Why would I kill Helen?"

"I don't know," Sarge said. "That's for the authorities to find out."

"I agree. Not some rent-a-cop."

"Now, Suze . . ." started Chad as he got to his feet.

"Miss Chase, it doesn't help to call people names."

Reynolds Pearce finally came to life, speaking from the entrance to the living room. "A lifeguard is supposed to trump a security guard? You've got to be kidding."

"I can't believe . . ." Jeremy stood, then shook his head. "Susan, how could you do something like this?"

"You didn't see anything, Jeremy," said Chad, "so watch your mouth."

"Easy for you to say." Our experience gatherer glanced at the dead woman illuminated by the candles and the gray light from the doorway. "You weren't close to Helen. I've just lost a dear friend."

Forgotten in all this was Vicki Hester who moaned.

Immediately, the investment banker was on a knee beside her. Reynolds looked up helplessly. "What do I do?"

Rent-a-cop said he would get a wet cloth and disappeared into the rear of the house.

"Well," said Jeremy, "you have to admit that finding you with the body is awfully damning."

"She was dead when I found her."

"Says you."

"That's good enough for me," Chad said.

"Of course," said Brandon from the door, "we'd expect you to stick up for your fiancée."

"That has nothing to do with it." Chad looked from one person to another in the flickering light. "There's more than one person in this house who wished harm would come to Helen."

Jeremy glanced at those in the room. "Name four."

My fiancé picked up the gauntlet. "You've been envious of the hold Helen has had over this crew since high school."

Jeremy grinned. "And the hold she held over you."

I looked at my fiancé.

"Suze, you know there was nothing between Helen and me."

I surveyed the room. Though no one moved, shadows flickered across the wall from the candles. "If today was any example, I'd say that Helen's been on all your cases for longer than you care to remember." I pointed at Reynolds Pearce who held Vicki Hester so she could sit up. "He still blames Helen for the loss of his job."

"It was the economy," protested Pearce. "We had invested heavily in the dot-coms and the axe had to fall on someone. I had the least seniority."

Chad said, "And you were the fool who thought his investment house should promote witchcraft."

When Reynolds stood, Vicki found she had to fend for herself. Very quickly her hands came out, palms down to hold herself upright.

"Could someone give me a hand?" she asked.

Sarge returned with a cloth he applied to the head of the now upright Vicki Hester.

"We were never going to promote witchcraft," Reynolds said. "It was an investment opportunity. Nothing more."

"And one that cost you your job." Next I took aim at Brandon Calhoun. "You as much as threatened Helen when I was with you on the porch."

"I did no such thing," said the LARPer, pushing back his black hat so the string caught around his neck. "You're saying that to make people think you didn't do it."

"I'm with Chad, remember? Honey, would you get my credentials? They're in my fanny pack in the bedroom."

As he turned to go, a puzzled Brandon murmured, "Credentials?"

Sarge helped Vicki to her feet. The woman held the cloth to her head, but her legs appeared wobbly.

Vicki cleared her throat. "Chad said you . . . you and Helen went back a ways."

"They were lifeguards," Jeremy said. "Susan as much as admitted this to me only minutes before . . . we found Helen." He looked at me. "Or she found her."

"So she says," added Reynolds Pearce.

"Wait a minute, wait a minute," said Chad from the doorway and beside our resident vampire. "Everything about Susan and Helen's relationship was of Helen doing the taking, not giving. That's why we're all here. We couldn't believe Helen McCuen would actually put her life at risk for the Grand Strand, a place she reviles on her web site as being akin to Sodom and Gomorrah."

"Look, folks," I said, holding up my hands, "if you want me to take responsibility for sticking the screwdriver in Helen's chest, so be it. But I couldn't've killed her."

Chad gaped. The others stared at me, not actually believing what they'd heard.

"Then you're saying you're guilty?" asked Sarge.

I shrugged. "It's a misdemeanor to mutilate a corpse."

Then came the questions:

"She wasn't killed by the screwdriver?"

I shook my head. "Not enough blood."

"Then how was she killed?"

"I have no idea. I haven't had a chance to examine the body."

"But isn't that Perry's job?"

"Perry's not qualified to examine a crime scene."

"And what makes you think you are?"

"I watch a lot of the Discovery Channel. Chad, would you please get my credentials?"

He left to do so, climbing the winding staircase on the run, thumping his way upstairs. Vicki Hester held onto Reynolds' arm with her free hand, the other still holding the cold compress to her forehead. Her face was ashen. She looked at Helen, then at Jeremy.

"How could you?" she asked.

"You see, Miss Chase—"

"Er—Sarge, Vicki's accusing Jeremy, not me."

Everyone looked at the bearded guy as I remembered that Helen had said Vicki was under Jeremy's thumb.

Our experience collector's hands came up in surrender. "Is this a game of hot potato? If so, we came through the door and found Susan hiding her handiwork."

His defense was lost, however, in the whistling of the wind through the open door. Everyone turned and stared when a loud boom rocked the house.

"Oh, I forgot to tell you," said our security expert. "While I was in the kitchen, the TV reported the return of the hurricane."

"Jeez, Susan," Reynolds said, "I wish you hadn't killed Helen. Now we're all going to die."

I think that's what he said. I'm not sure I heard him correctly. We were all making a mad dash for the front door. We stumbled onto the porch, near the railing, and held on tight. Not only was the wind up, but the wind threw water in our faces. It was *déjà vu* all over again.

There was no beach and the jetty was gone. Gray and white water slammed into the rocks protecting the berm. The murky liquid spilled over, tumbling into the yard and encroaching on the property, including the grassy area between the beach and the front of the house. The sky was dark, and clouds—dark and lighter ones—fought for mastery. The dark side seemed to be winning.

Sarge said, "We've got to secure the house again."

Vicki gripped the railing. "We're going to stay inside with a dead person?"

"I'll take Lady Light upstairs," Sarge said.

"That would be tampering with a crime scene."

"Miss Chase, I don't need a riot on my hands."

"Everyone can go to their rooms and wait to be interrogated."

"Interrogated? By whom?" Brandon bit his bloodless lip.

"Susan," said Jeremy, "just because you've found a few runaways doesn't mean we have to listen to accusations by some amateur detective."

"We have to get inside," seconded Reynolds Pearce.

Rain blew at the horizontal, hitting our skin like needles and forcing a vote. We all stumbled through the anteroom and into the hallway, damp, sweaty, and nervous. Lady Light still sat on the sofa.

I coughed and cleared my throat. I wanted to go to my room, lie down, and be held by Chad. Any moment I was going to break down and cry. Another person I had known was dead, and it reminded me of when a serial killer had once killed, mutilated, and posed my friends on the beach. People like Helen McCuen.

I swallowed back my tears. My emotions were catching up with me, which is probably why I had been such a bitch when it came to ex-sergeant Perry Jackson.

Sarge closed the front doors, then the second set. Wind tore at the building and rain hit the walls like a machine gun blast. It was all dawning on us that we were once again attending a hurricane party. If the ocean was over the berm, and if it ever got a foothold on the lower level, soon the surf would be sucking the guts out of the first floor. We looked at each other. All of us avoided looking into the living room.

I gripped a pocket door, then the other, closing us off from the dead woman. "I think we've seen quite enough of this."

"Are we going to our rooms?" asked Vicki, watching the darkness surround her once again. Flashlights began to reappear.

"Until I call you down for an interrogation."

"Susan," said Jeremy snapping on his light, "I really don't understand why you insist on doing Perry's job."

"I'm not answering any of your questions," Reynolds Pearce stated flatly.

"I have a room to myself . . ." said Vicki, glancing at the semidarkness surrounding around us. "I—I don't think I can stay in it alone."

Chad heard this as he came down the stairs. "You can stay with Susan and me."

Another bad idea from my knight in shining armor.

I snatched the wallet from his hand and opened the flap. Inside was a lousy picture, but it certified that I was an agent of SLED.

"You're with SLED?" asked more than one of the fools standing in the alcove.

"Yes, and now if you don't mind, I would prefer that everyone return to their rooms."

"I'm not cooperating with any cop," said Brandon.

"Nor do you have to," I said with a shrug, "but you will go to prison."

"Are you serious?" He gestured at the sound of the wind and the rain hammering on the east side of the house. "And just how are you going to enforce that?"

"Brandon, this time when the Horry County cops run you in, it'll be for more than disturbing the tourists. It's called obstruction of justice." I pocketed my wallet in my jeans. "Now," I added, slapping my hands together and drawing their attention. "Everyone to their rooms."

They looked at each other, then silently moved

upstairs. Sarge remained behind, but I told him to take a hike. I didn't want someone looking over my shoulder. He was told to head for the room Chad and I shared, once he made sure that Vicki Hester's room was secure.

"Chad, are you going to be able to help me?"

"Help?" He glanced at the closed doors to the living room. "What do you have to do?"

"I have to assess how she died. It wasn't from the screwdriver."

He nodded. "Doubt that it was or you wouldn't have said what you did."

"I was acting a bit idiotic." I glanced at the characters trudging up the winding staircase. "But I come by it easily, with all the idiots in this place."

"What do you want me to do?" His face was somber.

"I don't have my recorder, but there's a pen and paper in the kitchen. Get those and we'll start with Helen."

He glanced at the front doors. "Don't we have to do something about the storm?"

"What would that be? We're as buttoned up as—"

"Before Helen turned back the storm. Yes, I see." Chad left to fetch the notebook and pen.

I called after him. "And if you find some rubber gloves under the sink, bring them along."

Chad nodded that he would.

From upstairs, Sarge hollered over the sound of the wind and rain that Miss Hester's room was secure and he was headed for the one assigned to Chad and myself.

I pulled back the pocket doors. I wasn't worried about prints. Everyone's hands had to be on those doors. Except for Vicki, who didn't look as if she was strong enough to roll them out of the interior of the wall. Shutters rattled as rain shook the house. Damn if I wasn't attending another hurricane party, and this time I wasn't the least bit drunk.

Hurricane Hugo had been a category four, which means winds between 131 and 155 miles per hour, and all chance of escape, meaning the surface roads, are cut off by rising water three to six hours before the center of the storm arrives. It also means when the storm's waves come ashore, they are going to scuttle anything on the lower floors of any structure. Waves or floating debris do the actual work.

But the four of us weren't scuttled—ten before a lack of nerve and a higher IQ cut our motley crew down to four. I was the only girl, but, hey, this was going to be fun. I had a pack filled with an assortment of hiking food and several bottles of water. I also had in my possession a sleeping bag, a couple of extra towels, and a lantern. There was an extra flashlight in the bottom of the pack, along with a small first aid kit, and most of what I had was scrounged off those who took the last vehicle out of the Grand Strand. My contribution had been one of those new "suitcases" of beer; you know, eighteen to a carton. And I had some munchies. You might say I was clueless.

Luckily for us the house had been a two-story because when the water began to rise, we quickly found ourselves in the loft—if that qualifies as a two-story house. We happily sang "Ninety-nine Bottles of Beer on the Wall," drank said beer, ate the munchies, and listened to the wind howl and the waves batter the house. Everything was pretty cool until the house began to rock. Then move.

We had already suffered through cracking glass, though the windows had taped "Xs" across the panes and were shuttered with plywood. We had also survived anything not bolted down tumbling into the water filling the first floor. The lantern was one of those. The lantern had been at the head of the stairs, and down the stairs it tumbled, dripping camp fuel as it went.

Immediately the stairs were aflame, but one of the guys leaped into the water, and for his trouble, banged his knee on a submerged object. After a yelp, he began to use his hands like a kid in a swimming pool water fight. It wasn't long before the fire was doused, and the guy back in the loft, shivering. Since this was not my house, I thought all this great fun and figured the world moving around me was part of the buzz.

Then I realized the house was moving!

I gripped the arm of the boy to the left and to the right of me. My beer sat between my legs, and the more the house moved, the tighter my thighs squeezed together—and more liquid oozed through the opening in the lid and wet me.

Or had I wet myself? Hard to tell. The house had been shaken loose from its foundation, which was nothing more than a concrete slab, and turned into a grotesque amusement ride.

Under the pressure of the wind, all houses along Surfside Beach not pillared to the beach were slowly being moved across Ocean Boulevard. Our house skidded into the parking area behind it, then leveled the fence separating us from the road and scoured its way onto Ocean Boulevard and across it.

During all this, the first floor remained totally underwater, with the occasional piece of furniture bobbing to the surface. Still, the sounds of the storm disappeared—because we were screaming like we were going over the rise at the Pavilion's roller coaster.

I screamed for my mama or my daddy. Which was another sick joke. Daddy had hit mama one too many times, and she'd walked out on us when I was thirteen. So here I was, possibly never going to reach the ripe old age of sixteen because I didn't have parents to warn me to stay away from parties held during hurricanes.

Like that would've stopped me.

Tears ran down my cheeks, I gripped the arms of the guys next to me tighter, and sobbed into his shoulder as we rode in the Mad Hatter's teacup, plowing down everything in our path.

Finally, we jolted to a stop, but that didn't mean the tears and shaking stopped. Still, this was where we finished the storm, and when the ocean receded, we cautiously unlocked the door—one of the guys had to kick it open—and ventured into a gray and drizzly day.

Before we could starve to death, the National Guard came along, policed us up, and ferried us inland to where a shelter had been set up. Several people thought it their business to tell us how stupid, reckless, and what a generally lame thing we had done.

No need. I swore I'd never attend another hurricane party.

Until, that is, I fell for Chad Rivers.

"Where do we begin?" asked Chad, returning from the kitchen with the pen and pad.

"I want to move Helen to see if there's any blood."

He handed me the pink rubber gloves he'd taken from under the sink. They smelled of disinfectant as I put them on, struggling to get one of the fingers over my engagement ring. I stared at the ring. I was soon to be married. If I didn't get killed by the hurricane, or whoever had killed Helen McCuen.

"First note I want you to take . . ."

No acknowledgment from beside me. Chad was staring at Helen. He looked to be in pain.

"Chad, I need you to take notes. Or go upstairs and hold Vicki's hand."

My fiancé shook like a dog coming out of the water. "I'm—I'm okay."

"No, you're not, and neither am I, but we have a job to do."

"Why can't this wait until the storm blows over?"

I ticked points off on my pink fingers. "One, because the storm could damage the crime scene, and, two, Lieutenant Warden would have some serious questions about my nerve."

"Your nerve?"

"He already questions my sanity for being here. It'll probably put me on probation again."

Chad smiled rather weakly. "I didn't know you ever got off probation."

I ignored the crack. "Anyway, this notebook has to survive the storm and it can't get wet."

"I have extra baggies. You said there were other reasons?"

"I want the killer to know that there's a professional on duty, and not some rent-a-cop. That might be enough to deter him from killing again."

"He?"

"You don't really think Vicki killed Helen, do you?"

He shook his head. "Not for a moment. Vicki is here because Helen taunted her into coming."

"Pretty close to how she got everyone here. The exception would be Perry Jackson. Hon, you said you went to school with all these people at one time or another. When did you go to school with Perry Jackson?"

"I was trying to remember. Perry was at Conway High for a few months." Chad paused. The thought appeared to hurt his feelings.

"What's the problem?"

"Oh, nothing, Suze. I was just remembering high school."

"No fond memories?" I asked with a slight smile and kneeling in front of the sofa. I had shoved the coffee table out of the way.

"My mother was always pressing me to join a clique."

"And you were interested only in your boats?"

He nodded as he joined me on the floor in front of Helen.

"So Perry came and went."

"Joined the army, I guess. I remember his name from Operation Desert Storm. The paper printed all the names of those who'd gone in harm's way." Chad glanced at the winding staircase. "Who do you think did it? Perry, Jeremy, Reynolds, or Brandon?"

"I don't have an opinion. I just gather facts."

Then we got to work. I told him everything I observed about the body and Chad dutifully wrote it down.

When he had finished making a note, Chad said, "One thing about Vicki that's always bothered me."

"Yes?" I asked, straightening up.

"She's had lots of bad luck."

"Like what?"

"Her pets die, her car always breaks down, and none of her relationships work out."

"Did you have one with her?"

"Suze!"

"Sorry. None of my business. How do you know all this?"

"She didn't live in our subdivision. Her family

couldn't afford it. I don't think we could either, but mother insisted."

"What was her family like?"

"Five girls. Her father was a fireman, her mother worked as a receptionist or a secretary."

"Four girls as siblings means there wasn't a lot of money to go 'round, and it's tough be the center of attention."

"Wait a minute, wait a minute. You think Vicki killed her pets to get attention?"

"Chad, why would that be the first thought that came to mind?"

"I don't know. But I'll have to admit it was the first thought that entered my mind."

"Try this on for size: what kind of guys did she date? Don't think. Just describe them in one word."

"Losers."

I nodded. "Some families are disaster-prone. They put themselves in situations by how they handle their affairs so that disaster always strikes. Did Vicki's family strike you as being that way?"

He shook his head. "Not in the least."

"Then what better way to stand out than to become a witch."

"That would work," he said, nodding. "It has to cramp your love life if guys know you're a witch."

"Dead pets, broken cars, and bad love affairs can get you a lot of sympathy." I paused. "Like trying to get her hooks into you."

"Suze, she never had a chance."

"I know that now, but if a person wanted to be the center of attention, and in this house she had to compete with Lady Light, the time would be before and after the attempt to turn back the storm. When Vicki saw that her kissing and hugging got a rise out of me, she played to that, and the other guys watched. I know Jeremy enjoyed watching."

"Then you don't see her doing this." Chad inclined his head toward the body on the sofa.

I shook my head. "Vicki's simply a whining little girl who wanted to stand out in a family of five girls."

"You really are hard on families, aren't you?"

"We'll create our own. I've sorted through enough families to know what I want. They're on display every summer at the beach."

"Funny, you never mentioned this to me."

"Because you're hung up on my relationship with your mother." I gestured at the dead woman on the sofa where Jeremy had dropped the screwdriver.

Chad pulled back the folds of the dead woman's dress. "Er—Suze, there's no screwdriver."

"Yes," I said, looking at the dry vomit puddled up in the dead woman's lap. "I suppose the killer has it."

We scanned the room. The Phillips screwdriver was nowhere to be seen. We walked from one piece of furniture, looked under each, and came up empty.

"Make a note."

He did.

I returned to the red velvet sofa, whose color didn't help, and got on my hands and knees. No blood, nor did I see any shell casing. I didn't think Helen had been shot. No smell of cordite, but that could be masked by incense and candles. All of this Chad dutifully wrote down.

Leaning over Helen, I checked her neck. Feeling the thorax, I found everything intact. Nothing on the back of her neck. Nothing wrong with her neck, so our resident vampire didn't suck the blood from her body. No contusions, no bruises. No rigidity, still I didn't want to drop the body, which was now more or less a dead weight, no pun intended nor disrespect to the dead.

"Help me, Chad."

He put his pad and pen on the coffee table and asked what I wanted him to do.

"I want you to hold her so she doesn't fall one way or the other. I need to examine her back."

He did, and I learned Helen had not been knifed or otherwise stabbed.

"Then how did she die?"

"There could be a needle mark I can't see. Hell, she might've even overdosed."

"Helen's been clean for years. At least as long as she's been a witch." When I stared at him, he explained. "It's on her web site." He looked at Helen again. "Think she was poisoned?"

"Then why is no one else dead?"

"You tell me. You're the investigating officer. And what's this screwdriver bit? Is it because the killer didn't want us to notice the needle mark, if there is one? He inserted the needle in Helen's heart and killed her. You know, pushed in air."

"Anything's possible until there's an autopsy."

"But you knew for a fact the screwdriver did not kill her."

"Not enough blood. Someone walked through the room, plunged the screwdriver at her heart, and missed. When we figure out how she was killed, that will tell us who the killer is."

"I don't understand . . . ."

"Neither do I, but the screwdriver was a screw up."

"And now it's gone."

"Yes. So much for my ability to protect the integrity of a crime scene."

Once again, Chad smiled weakly. "More problems from Lieutenant Warden?"

"For sure."

"Suze, I'm not sure I can do this."

"Are you kidding," I said with a smile. "I couldn't sit long enough to sketch a ketch."

His smile grew stronger. "You're just saying that so I'll feel better."

"It's the truth." I leaned across the dead woman and kissed him. "What I need you to do now is to set up the ritual room for interrogation."

"You're going to interrogate each one separately?"

"It's my job."

He glanced at the front of the house where it sounded like the storm had definitely returned. Wind flailed the house with water. "How much time do you need?"

"Who knows, but you could help by placing one chair on either side of the former altar. Remove any extraneous material. Stash that stuff in the study across the hall and let me know when the room's ready."

I spent a few more minutes with Helen, said a few Hail Marys, and when Chad called to me, I had him head for the kitchen and put the coffee on, but only after inviting the first suspect to the ritual room.

"Who?"

"Sarge."

"You think he did it?"

"I don't know, Chad—"

He smiled. "You just gather facts."

Then, once Chad began his climb up the winding staircase, I pulled back the pocket door separating the ritual room from the living room—so that Helen McCuen could make her presence felt during each and every interview.

Chapter 9

Our security guard sat across the table from me, back to the hallway. It didn't appear to bother him.

"Sarge, how do you know these people?"

"I don't know them. You weren't listening, Miss Chase. You have that problem when your fiancé's around."

Swallowing my anger, I said through gritted teeth, "So tell me again."

"My company assigned me to this job. I was to make sure the building was secure, including the house being shuttered, provisions stored away, proper medical gear, and so on."

"You asked for this job?"

"I said I was assigned."

"When the storm is over, I'm going to check your story."

He squirmed in his chair.

"Well . . . ?"

"Okay, okay, I asked for the job."

"Why, for God's sake?" I glanced in the direction of the storm that surrounded the house once again.

"Looks good on one's resume."

"That you remained for a hurricane?"

He shook his head. "The preparations."

"So there was no formal request for you to remain behind, just as Helen said?"

"But I couldn't run off and leave—"

"The women and children."

"There are no children."

I didn't say I thought all the men were acting rather childish, and that Perry Jackson was engaged in the same pissing contest.

"You don't place women in dangerous situations." His arm swept out. "All the people in this house, they knew better."

"Including the women?"

That stopped him. He appeared to have left me, you know, like having fallen through the rabbit hole. On my part, I had simply reacted like an insulted feminist and almost missed his meaning.

"You're not talking about this party, are you?" I asked.

"Sure . . . ." He found the floor between his feet rather fascinating.

"Spit it out, Sergeant."

He was quiet for a long moment, readying himself to tell the truth. Or another lie.

He looked up and leaned forward, placing his huge forearms on the table in front of the flickering candle.

"You know about the American women taken prisoner during Desert Storm? The ragheads raped one of them."

"This woman who was raped was a soldier?"

"Of course."

"What about it? She knew the dangers when she

joined up." That was my inherent feminism raising its ugly head again and causing me to miss an important clue.

"Miss Chase, you don't put women in harm's way."

I wanted to laugh, but Lieutenant Warden would not consider that professional. I don't know why I wanted to impress Warden so much. He wasn't my boss any more.

"You're denying women the same right to make fools of themselves by attending a hurricane party?"

He sat back in his chair and nodded. "That's why I remained behind."

Thinking it was time to get on with the interrogation, I asked, "Tell me, Sarge, where were you when Helen was murdered?"

"On the porch with the others."

"How do you know that's where you were when she died?"

"It's obvious. Someone passed through the room, perhaps leaned down to hand her something, or make a gesture of friendship, and slammed the screwdriver into her chest, and was gone."

"Perry, the screwdriver didn't kill her."

"Then how . . . ?" He sat there, considering. "The lack of blood?"

"And what else?"

He thought for a moment, and as he did, he stared at the upright Helen McCuen on the red velvet sofa. When Jackson got to his feet, I did, too, but I didn't follow him into the adjoining room.

At the sofa, he bent over the corpse, and then checked her neck and her back as I had done. He even slid a hand under the dead woman's body.

"No blood for sure."

"And her mouth?"

"The moisture's crystallized, but I think there were bubbles when we found her." He looked at me from the other room. "Vomit?" He gestured at the woman's lap.

I nodded and returned to my seat in the adjoining room.

Perry leaned over and studied the darkish spot on the bodice, then straightened up and left Helen where she sat. He returned to the interrogation chair. "You're thinking poison?"

"Actually I'm listening to you."

"But if she wasn't stabbed or shot, it has to be poison."

"If it *was* poison, then who would've had the opportunity to use that poison?"

"Well," he said, becoming comfortable with his role as my Watson, "anyone who had access to whatever Miss McCuen drank or ate."

"Do you know of anything she drank or ate that was different from what anyone else drank or ate?"

"Can't say I can. Of course, when you use arsenic, it could have been done over a period of time, then a final dose administered."

"When?"

"At dinner."

"And who made sure everyone was served seconds?" I asked with a small smile.

He sat up. "Miss Chase, I did not kill the woman in the other room."

"If not you, which of these people had the opportunity?"

"Anyone could've done it."

"How does that help us develop the case?"

He bit his lip. "Okay. Figure it happened in the last few hours, the final dose, that is. I was in the kitchen like everyone else. I was watching the progress of the storm and wondering if my job was over. When I work on a job, Miss Chase, I tune out the distractions. You can't get machinery working in a combat zone if you're not concentrating on the job at hand."

"You gave us the impression you were a rifleman. What kind of machinery would a person in a rifle company have to repair?"

Glancing at the floor, he said, "I never made it into combat."

I leaned forward. "Because the army gave you an aptitude test and learned of your potential ability to fix and repair machinery."

He nodded.

I smiled. "You REMFs are all the same."

The surprise showed on his face. "You know about REMFs?"

"I've dated soldiers from Columbia and the former Myrtle Beach Air Force Base. To an experienced combat soldier, such as those from Fort Jackson, all Air Force personnel were REMFS or 'rear echelon mother . . . ,' well, you know what I mean—guys who never saw combat but are assigned duties in the rear."

I leaned back in my chair. "And you want to deny women the right to serve on the front lines? Why's that, Perry? Because you missed your opportunity to get your butt shot off?"

"Like I told you, Miss Chase, there are some places women don't belong."

And back through the rabbit hole we fell. "A few minutes ago you said everyone knew that. That would include the women, wouldn't it?"

Sarge said nothing, only stared at the floor. I had caught him in two inconsistencies and he was looking for wiggle room. I appeared to let him off the hook by asking, "Tell me about yourself, Perry."

"Huh?" He looked up. "What's there to tell? I'm an army brat."

"Any brothers or sisters?"

He glanced at the floor.

"What's the problem, Jackson?" When demanding information from a military type, it's best to call them by their surname. It's what they're used to.

"I was in school all over the world. I was in Germany, Japan, just about anywhere that had an Air Force base that allowed dependents."

"Where did you attend high school?"

"Lots of places."

"I mean in the States."

He sat there, staring at the floor. "My dad was in the Air Force so it was all over."

"So he served at Myrtle Beach Air Force Base." Where people in this day and age fly in for a weekend of golf and middle-aged debauchery. "Have any brothers or sisters?"

"One sister," he said in a soft voice.

"Older or younger?"

"Younger. Much younger." He glanced in the direction of the dead Helen McCuen. "Look, Miss Chase, I need to tell you what it's like to be a kid in the military."

"I'm listening."

"Well, there are three groups."

"Go on."

"One group—I don't know how many there are in each group by percentage, but one groups buys into the program."

"Program?"

"They like their father being in the military."

"And there are two more."

"Those who don't like it, and you can spot them with the dyed hair, tattoos, and earrings."

"And the third group?"

"Never have the nerve to make the move to one group or the other so they just hang back."

"And this has to do with the death of Helen McCuen how?"

"I was in the group who bought into the program. My sister was on the bubble."

"So?"

"So we attended Conway High School with some of the same people in this house."

"Why would you do that?"

"My folks were divorcing because my old man always avoided stateside duty. My mother said she'd get a job—she was computer-trained and that was a big deal back then if you could do spreadsheets. Lotus One, Two, Three, and all that stuff. We lived in Conway and my father lived on base."

"How long were you there?"

"Less than a semester. I graduated and joined up."

"That's what you mean about 'buying into the program'?"

He visibly straightened in his chair. "My father was very proud of me."

"But your mother was disappointed, and she put pressure on your sister to belong to a social group."

He nodded, the pride turning into sadness.

"What's wrong with that?"

"You could say it drove her mad and ultimately killed her."

That made no sense, so I asked, "Binge drinking or sex without protection?"

"No, Miss Chase, it was something your fiancé had a hand in."

I had to take a breath. "I think you're going to have to explain that."

"Ask your fiancé if he remembers Dolly Jackson."

"I will, but I'd like to hear your side of the story."

"You think I'm BS-ing you?"

"The thought did cross my mind."

"And why would I do that?"

"Because you killed Helen McCuen."

"What would be my motivation?"

"You schemed your way into this house. I simply have to figure out why."

"I received a letter. It informed me if I was interested in seeing all the people who had had a hand in the death of my sister, I should be here. The note said, with my connections, there shouldn't be any problem with me hooking up with Lady Light."

"You think Helen sent you the invite?"

The former sergeant merely shrugged.

"Helen might've wanted you to see the others and how they reacted to your presence." I crossed my legs. "Speaking of that, how did my fiancé and the others kill this sister of yours?"

"You know a place called Waties Island?"

"It's not much of an island. Just a place where dumb-asses sometimes get trapped when the tide comes in."

He gave me a grim smile.

I wanted to make sure I was hearing him correctly.

"Your sister was left on Waties Island overnight?"

"By everyone in this house."

"Including Chad?"

"It was his boat that was used."

"And his motivation would be?"

"To be part of the clique."

"Sarge, I can honestly tell you that you and I are talking about two different people."

Jackson sat up, leaned forward, and put his huge

forearms on the table once again.

I drew up my legs.

He saw the motion. "Now, don't get your panties in a wad, Miss Chase. Dolly just wanted to be part of a group."

"And the only way you could join the clique was through an initiation?"

"You catch on fast." The pock-marked face smiled. "I just might believe you are an agent of SLED."

"I don't care what you believe as long as you don't obstruct justice."

"I'm talking, aren't I? More than I ever thought. Probably more than I should."

"It does give you a motive to kill any number of people in this house."

"Yes, it does, I'm sorry to say." In the light from the candle on the former altar, I could see his hands clenching. "Dolly was told someone would stay with her. They lied. They abandoned her out there, and your fiancé was one of them."

"Just for the sake of argument, tell me how they got your sister there?"

"Dolly thought they were going for a boat ride and picnic. Perhaps smoke some dope, maybe someone would try to put a move on her. They were paired up."

"Everyone in this house was there, you say?"

"Yes."

"Then they were not paired up, Sarge. There are four men and three women, if you include your sister."

Sarge looked ill-at-ease. It was probably the first time he'd done the math.

"And once left behind, Dolly thought she couldn't return to the mainland?"

"Yeah."

"There's a causeway. Your sister could have returned to the mainland by using the causeway." When he didn't reply, I said, "Perry, your story doesn't hold together, like several other parts of our conversation. If my fiancé was involved, like you said, why would he need a boat? You can wade out to Waties Island."

Another smile from the pock-marked man. "Now that all depends on whether the tide's in or out, doesn't it, Miss Chase."

"Reynolds, are you going to tell me why you're really here?"

The investment banker glanced at Helen in the other room after sitting down. "You already know what the witch did to my company."

"Reynolds, if you don't start cooperating, you're not going back to Charlotte."

The chunky man shrugged. "I've got no reason to return. Word gets around. I might as well move to New York and start all over again."

"Because of what Helen did."

"Of course," he said, in the flickering light from the candle.

"You think she destroyed your life."

"I was doing Helen a favor. I touted her plan to the board and they laughed in my face."

"Helen thought there was more to it than that."

"That's because I made her *think* I was doing more."

"So her idea was—"

"DOA. No way any investment firm is going to be known for promoting witchcraft."

"But you strung it out, making Helen think she had a shot."

"But I didn't kill her, even though she thoroughly

botched working in Charlotte for me. Now I'll have to return to New York."

"That's so bad?"

"I was there on 9/11."

Nodding, I said, "Oh, yeah. I remember the story."

When terrorists flew into the World Trade Center, Reynolds was working for a firm in one of the adjoining buildings. The way Reynolds tells the story, on that particular day he was headed for work, late again because he hated New York and had his résumé circulating down south. Reynolds so loved Charlotte that he would fly home weekends to the place where he'd gotten his start in investment banking, and while the Queen City might be small potatoes to those in the Big Apple, Charlotte ranks second in investment banking only to New York.

On 9/11, Reynolds was hustling toward his glass building when the first plane went into the first tower. Reynolds stopped and looked up. It appeared that terrorists had finally figured out how to detonate a bomb in the World Trade Center. The car bomb that had been set off in the garage, years earlier, had been, comparatively speaking, a snafu. While passers-by stopped to watch the show, another plane rammed into the second tower.

Reynolds said he grabbed a guy and gal and hustled them inside a building across the street. Good that he did. Soon pieces of planes, buildings, and bodies were showering the street where they had once stood. Reynolds returned home within a week, and since his firm had no office in Charlotte, they gracefully let him go.

"I don't see how you know so much about me," said Reynolds, squirming around in his chair.

In a singsong voice, I said, "The old-fashioned methods of accounting weren't set up to monitor the performance of the modern-day company. Those methods undervalue companies because research and development are expensed for the current fiscal year, though current R&D affects the future of the company, just as a building is depreciated. R&D, advertising costs, such as trademarks, should all be proportionally depreciated over a period of years, and the same goes for the training of personnel. Straight depreciation, not accelerated depreciation, will properly evaluate the value of a company, not earnings per share."

The investment banker leaned forward on the former altar, his eyes wet with excitement. "I didn't know you understood . . . ."

"Dammit, Reynolds, I don't even know what I said, but I've heard it over the back of booths at Johnny Rocket's, between selections at Dueling Pianos, and on the boardwalk near the Pavilion. It's enough to make me wonder if your firm fired you for being a big fat bore."

"No, no," he said, shaking his head. "Over three hundred companies worldwide use this new method of accounting."

"Maybe that's why Enron collapsed."

"You've got that all wrong. Enron's debt-to-equity ratio was too high. Actually, with Enron's decentralized structure, an employee might know of a problem in one area but not another, and if you pointed out a problem, you became the problem."

"Enough!" I sat up. Jeez! I needed a drink. So I drank from the coffee cup Chad had provided between interviews. After a long sip, I asked, "Reynolds, why was Chad reading you guys the riot act on the porch?"

He sat back in his chair. Carelessly, he tossed his hand. "It was nothing."

"Where was Sarge while this was going on?"

"Huh? He was on the porch. Not with us, but around the corner."

"So what was this 'nothing' that Chad was so worked up about?"

"He was blowing off at Jeremy as he usually does." Reynolds glanced in the other room. "When Helen's not around."

"Don't wander, Reynolds. Be specific."

He smiled. "You don't like their history, do you? It gets under your skin."

I leaned forward in my chair. "Okay, Reynolds, you want to talk history. Let's talk history. Remember a girl by the name of Dolly Jackson? She was left on Waties Island at the same time you attended Conway High School."

His face lost its smile, and, he, too, began to stare at the floor.

Waties Island is part of the Northern Strand and the Grand Strand is a long sliver of overgrown tourist traps from Murrells Inlet to Cherry Grove. Waties Island is what is called a coastal island, and if you don't mind getting your feet wet, you can walk the fifty or so yards to the island. There's also a causeway, not much of a road, but the causeway wasn't something this crew was going to tell Dolly Jackson about.

Still, Waties is a legitimate island, with pines, sand dunes, and sea turtle nests studied by Coastal Carolina. It contains two burial mounds. Harry Poinsett once told me Indians have this quaint custom of dropping a rock or pebble on a burial mound as they pass by, but because shells were more common at the beach, they'd drop those as they passed by. The mounds are supposed to be haunted, but, hey, what're a few ghosts after a witch has turned back a hurricane.

I said, "Dolly Jackson wasn't told about the causeway that had been recently built from the mainland to the island, was she?"

Rain hit the side of the house like carpenters working against a deadline and with both hands filled with nail guns. The candle flickered, illuminating the blond man's hair as he stared at his feet.

I leaned back in my chair, wanting to be as far away as possible from this blond-headed monster. "What makes this worse is your crew did this knowing that, years ago, two teenagers took a boat from Little River Neck to where some hermit lived along the coast. Those boys went to prison, not for armed robbery, but for murdering an old man when he didn't give up the loot they believed he had hidden in his shack."

Reynolds continued to stare at the floor.

"And knowing there are such predators along the Grand Strand, you still left that girl out there."

He was still silent, unable to meet my eyes.

"And your crew made damn sure Dolly knew if she attempted to swim to the mainland, she'd drown. The water's treacherous when the tide's in—that's what you told her—and since it was springtime, no one would be on the mainland to hear the girl's cries."

Reynolds head snapped up. "What's the big deal? Chad took a boat out and returned her to shore."

Chapter 10

I shook a finger at Reynolds. "If you're jerking my chain, so help me—"

Still the smile. "You don't think your fiancé could be part of something like that?"

Leaning forward, I said, "I sure as hell don't."

He continued to grin like the Cheshire cat. "You know Chad has history with both Helen and Vicki."

"Reynolds, don't go there."

"Chad would do anything . . ." He stopped, seeing something in my gray-blue eyes. They say looks can kill, and when I have bad days it appears my eyes can transmit that message.

"Give it up, Reynolds. And stick to the facts."

He cleared his throat. "Well, Vicki told Chad she heard a voice calling for help. From the island."

"Told him? What are you talking about? You said Chad was at the party."

"Well, he arrived somewhat late."

"Reynolds, cut the crap. I want to know what you think you're telling me."

"Vicki called Chad and said she hadn't been able to roust anyone out of their house because it was out of season. You know how it is. Chad's always taking up Vicki's slack."

"Then your crew did leave Dolly Jackson on Waties Island."

"No, no," he said, shaking his head. "We just went out and picked her up."

I felt my eyes narrow. "How'd you know she was there?"

"We just knew . . . ."

"You knew? I don't think so! You jerks planned the whole thing, like a snipe hunt."

He sat there, appearing mournful, feeling sorry for himself, certainly not for Dolly Jackson.

"With the outgoing tide, you had only a twelve-hour opportunity to scare the hell out of this girl, which probably means all five of you hung together because it wouldn't be any fun—laughing, drinking, and making sick jokes about what it must be like to be trapped on an island in the middle of the night." I glanced around the darkened room with its weird and funny shadows caused by the lighting. "You stayed here with that redhead—"

"Wendy Archibald was never part of our group. She had no idea what was going on."

"So none of you went with Chad because Wendy would've known something was up. Maybe something she'd like to have been a part of, and if she wasn't allowed to participate, then you guys might lose the use of this house if she actually discovered your group was using her."

Once again he retreated into silence, and I could hear the rain flogging the house—from the south. Hurricane winds are from the direction of the storm, and Lili was coming from the east. Had to be some very serious gusts outside this house.

"Were any of you there when Chad brought Dolly ashore?"

No answer to this either.

"Reynolds, I'm going to get to the bottom of this with or without your help, and someone is going to prison for what was done to that girl."

"Actually . . . actually, we didn't know where Chad would bring her ashore."

"Did you or any of your clique go see her? At the hospital? During Dolly's recovery?"

"Well, I did have a job interview in Charlotte, working as an intern between my junior and senior year."

"I'm beginning to not like that town."

"What's there not to like?"

I wanted to tell him that a friend of mine had been raped, robbed, and murdered in the parking lot of a shopping mall south of the Queen City.

"The Waties Island incident was what Chad was reading you guys the riot act about, wasn't it? He finally figured out why everyone was summoned here."

Reynolds began to stare at the hardwood floor again. "I don't want to talk about Waties Island."

I pressed him, now leaning on the former altar. "Lifeguards, emergency workers, and even plain tourists have to go out and bring people ashore. Close to twelve hours can seem like an eternity when you can't find the causeway, or in Dolly's case, didn't know it existed. Most fools trapped there are tourists. They don't know jack about tides and forget what comes in, must go out. Or they get impatient or panic."

I straightened up and stared at the blond-headed, square-shouldered man across the table. When he looked up, it was my turn to smile. "Know anyone with the name of 'Jackson' in this house? Someone who might be Dolly's older brother?"

Next up was our resident vampire.

Brandon Calhoun cast long shadows because he didn't immediately sit down. After glancing at Helen in the living room, he said, "I didn't do anything. You can ask anybody. I was with someone all the time."

"Who?"

"Not who, but where."

Crossing my legs and wishing I had a cigarette, I asked, "Now what does that mean?"

"I was on the porch. People were with me all the time."

"Who was there when I left you? I didn't see anyone."

Our vampire pursed his lips. "In a few minutes Reynolds came out. He—he could've been the one to kill her. He's the one with the grudge. Helen put a curse on his investment firm."

I said nothing.

"And there's Jeremy," added the fellow who so much wanted to look like a modern-day vampire.

"What would be Jeremy's motive?"

"Helen McCuen upstaged him all the time."

"That's a reason to murder someone?"

"Ask Vicki. Ask Chad. Jeremy and Helen have been waging this contest to see who can become the most famous."

"That's why you dropped out and went into role-playing in the street."

"Look, Susan, I know you don't understand LARP, but it's my thing. Can't you leave it alone?"

"Not if it helps me understand Helen and Jeremy."

Brandon sat down and slumped in the chair. His long legs came out in front of him as he scooted his rump forward to the edge.

"All five of you were in the same race, weren't you?"

Brandon only stared at his boots.

"You ran in the same circle: Helen, Jeremy, Reynolds, Vicki, and you. All competing as to who would make it the farthest from Conway, and none of you were gifted athletes or blessed with superior intellectual gifts."

Brandon looked up.

"Going through high school, you became aware of each other, hung together, and bragged about how you were going to shake off the dust of Conway and never return."

"We're back," said our live action role player with a thin line of a smile. "How does that fit into your plan?"

"Because of your common goal."

"Oh," he said with a sneer, "to do more than marry, have babies, and a mortgage like you and Chad."

"Brandon, the rest of your former crew passed you up long ago, but still you came to the party, and remained here because you want to make sure everyone keeps the secret about what you did to Dolly Jackson."

He scooted back from me.

"But don't worry," I reassured him. "Dolly won't tell. She's still babbling. You guys really did a number on her."

His feet drew up under him. He sat up. "I—I don't know what you're talking about."

"Waties Island."

He shook his head a little too quickly. "Doesn't ring a bell."

"I have witnesses who will swear—"

Brandon stood, pushing back the chair. "I don't care what anyone says. I had nothing to do with that."

As his pale face turned red, I was practically on the balls of my feet sitting across from him.

"Susan, why can't you just leave me alone? You don't know what it's like to be persecuted. I can't play my games on the street without people making fun of me or calling the cops."

"Brandon, you're almost thirty. Don't you think you should find something beside those silly games and selling comic books?"

"Who are you to judge? You're a damn lifeguard!"

"Was."

"So you say." He glanced at my jeans. "Those credentials could be fake."

"Then why didn't you leave when you had the chance?" I leaned forward, resting my arms on the table. "When I ran into you on the porch, you were trying to make up your mind whether to leave or not. Blowing off at me about Helen was your frustration talking."

"I am not frustrated! You don't know anything about me."

Very calmly I said, "You were frustrated at being scared to leave, and it had nothing to do with the hurricane. You had a chance to leave after Helen banished the storm, but you chose to stay. Which allowed my fiancé to read you guys the riot act about what you had done to Dolly Jackson."

When he didn't move, I added, "Sit down, Brandon. We're not finished."

"I don't know what you're talking about, Susan."

"Sit down!"

Reluctantly, he took the seat across the table from me again.

"There are five people in this house who have good cause to kill Helen."

He tried to say something, but I held up my hand. "Let's say a harmless little man . . ." I stopped. "A harmless tall man finds himself in the wrong place at the wrong time. A person like that could come forward and tell all. He'd have no reason to hold back. It could do nothing to his reputation. But it's not that easy for a man of mystery. It's hard to give up that kind of respect. A man of mystery might be caught up in a role he's cursed to play out, when it actually might be better if he let it all hang out."

I canted my head. "I don't know how it plays out in prison, Brandon. If the mystery man has something extremely odd about him, he can keep the other perverts away. But . . . ." I gestured with an open palm. "What if the other perverts play along? Our man of mystery could have serious problems. In prison, that is."

Brandon was again slumped in his chair, feet and boots extended. "I've got nothing to say."

"Of course not. You don't have the guts."

Back again went the chair sliding across the floor as Brandon leaped to his feet. As it approached the hallway, the chair lost its balance and landed on its back.

"I think I'll leave now." He spoke pretty calmly for someone with red spots on both cheeks.

"Everyone's to remain here until the National Guard arrives, which should be the day after tomorrow. Then I'll turn the killer over to them."

"You know . . . who killed Helen?"

"I have a pretty good idea, but I could only share that information with someone I really trust."

"You don't think it's me?"

I shook my head.

"What do you want me to do?"

"You might begin by telling me your role in the Dolly Jackson snipe hunt."

"Snipe hunt?"

"A game older children play on younger ones. Give the new kid a bag, take them into the woods, and tell them to find a snipe. Tell them the birds are everywhere and quite tame, and the first one back wins a prize."

The pale face smiled, the red of his lips revealing the beginning of the fangs. He nodded. "There is no such bird. The game is a trick."

Gesturing at the chair on the floor behind him, I said, "Pull up a chair and tell me about Dolly Jackson. Then, and only then, I might believe you didn't have anything to do with Helen's death."

He stared at me for a long moment, then set the chair upright and fit his lanky frame back into it. "I'm relieved to hear you don't think I'm the killer."

"Others will be skeptical. We have to prove them wrong. Did you know there were two marks on Helen's neck," I lied, "like she'd been bitten?"

Our live action role player gulped. Any remaining color drained from his face. "Bite marks?"

"Just like the incisors you have."

"Someone's trying to set me up, Susan."

"And who would that be?"

"Reynolds, Jeremy, or Vicki."

"Not Chad? Or the Sarge?"

Brandon shook his head. "Chad's never been a part of our crowd. Sarge. I don't know him."

"It was his sister you left on Waties Island."

"You're kidding me." Our resident vampire glanced over his shoulder in the direction of the hall.

"That's why he's here. Did you invite him?"

"How could I invite him if I didn't know him?"

"He got a message from someone in this house."

"He could be lying."

"Anyone could be lying about any part of this." I smiled. "Even me."

Brandon again glanced over his shoulder toward the hall. "Do you think Jackson's here to kill us?"

"Well, he conveniently has all of you in one place."

Brandon was lost in thought, probably imagining all sorts of horrors some ex-soldier might do to his puny body. This guy had spent his life living vicariously through the activities of superheroes in graphic comic books. His imagination was running wild, and I did nothing to round it up. Sometimes there's a free energy in a case, and you have to use it or lose it.

"Now that Helen's out of the way," Brandon said, "he'll do the rest of us."

"Meaning who?"

"The ones who tricked his sister."

"You think he wouldn't be satisfied with just one? Say the ringleader, if it were Helen."

"There were always two leaders in our crowd," said the man in black, "and they fought like husband and wife." Leaning forward and using his bony hands to grip the edge of the table, he said, "You've got to bring us all together, Susan." His voice trailed off as he looked over his shoulder once again. His head snapped around to face me. "The kitchen. Jackson's not going to try anything with everyone together."

"He might poison us," I suggested, feeding this fool's fears. "To get rid of any potential witnesses. Jackson's the one with the ride, you know, the street-legal armored personnel carrier, and his company will back up his story that he was to have left before the storm arrived. Who's to say he didn't, if all of us are dead and washed out to sea."

I found myself enjoying frightening someone who made it his stock and trade to scare the bejesus out of soccer moms or anyone who happened to get in the way of a LARPs' constant search for the touchstone.

"Remember how Jackson has come and gone to the kitchen? All the food could be filled with poison."

"Then we won't eat."

"There are those munchies of Vicki's on the top of the refrigerator. Now that Helen's dead, she isn't in a position to object."

"Yeah," he said, nodding. "We should be able to hold out until the storm passes." He stood. "Why don't you organize this thing?"

Instead I leaned back in my chair, taking my coffee cup with me. "And why don't you tell me what happened the night you and the others took Dolly Jackson to Waties Island?"

"That's old news. What we've got to do is protect ourselves from Perry Jackson. He's a former soldier. No telling how many weapons he's got hidden in the house."

Jeez. I'd really done a job on this clown, and it was a few minutes before he was calm enough to sit down and tell me what happened.

"Dolly was new in town, young and impressionable. We were the local 'outsiders,' " said Brandon, referring to the book that had been required reading because teachers thought teenagers could learn from life in the fast lane.

"Did you know Dolly hated her name? Said there were only two variations: Dolly and Doll, which is what her father called her. She worshiped her father and hated being separated from him."

According to Brandon, Dolly was disoriented by the outside world. "All that overseas duty, you know. Dolly liked to stay on the base. She was very timid, and the wrong person to fall into the hands of Jeremy and Helen."

You want to be part of our crew, said Helen McCuen, you've got to spend the night on Waties Island.

Yes, chimed in Jeremy, once a year, before the tourists arrive, we wade out to Waties Island with beer and chips and camp among the Indian burial grounds. And tell ghost stories. We tell very gory ghost stories to see who can stand it. We want to know who can hang in there.

First one to bail was Reynolds. He appeared to cramp up crossing the three-foot-deep fifty yards of ocean separating the island from the mainland. Helen McCuen clapped Dolly on the shoulder and told her it appeared there'd be a new face in the group.

Reynolds Pearce had not cramped up. The clique was cutting down their numbers, and giving the new girl something to look forward to. Now, all she had to do was be able to withstand a bunch of ghost stories.

The next to go was Brandon Calhoun, then Vicki Hester. Brandon lurked around the campsite in the darkness waiting to go ashore, but Vicki hung on Helen's every word until her nerve appeared to snap and she ran for the mainland.

No moon, no fire, absolute darkness, and someone would reverse the batteries in Dolly's flashlight before leaving her behind. Brandon remembered that night for another reason. Helen and Jeremy had mocked him, saying he should have some work done on his teeth. Brandon thought maybe they were going too far and he considered warning Dolly.

Yeah. Right.

Brandon disappeared in the company of Vicki Hester. So did Jeremy in a mock fight with Helen. Dolly had seen them quarreling. This had gone on all week, and Brandon wondered, after the crack about his teeth, if things were getting out of hand between those two.

Helen poured it on with more gory stories. Brandon thought one was a Stephen King original but couldn't be sure. Finally there were only the two of them sitting on one of the Indian burial grounds, Helen regaling Dolly with tales of Captain Kidd and Blackbeard, who had each sought shelter in the coves and inlets around Little River. Some say treasure had been buried there, and time permitting, in the morning, perhaps they'd go searching for it. If the ghost of a pirate or an Indian didn't get them first. And all the time, Helen had to be consulting the luminous dial on her watch, seeing how many minutes she had to return to the mainland before the waters rose with the incoming tide.

Helen told the naïve teen that not only had pirates sailed along this coast, but also smugglers, Civil War blockade-runners, and modern-day drug dealers. Little River wanted to be known for its deep-sea fishing and Blue Crab festival, but Helen stuck to the darker side. Then, somewhere near midnight, slipping through the darkness of the pines and sliding across a final sand dune, Helen disappeared while Dolly answered a 'call of nature.'

Whether their victim was throwing up or pissing in her pants was not known. Helen, Brandon, Jeremy, and Vicki all left the island together and were met by Reynolds Pearce, who had returned with the car. To cover their tracks, Jeremy called Dolly's house and left word with her mother, saying they hadn't told their new friend the party was off.

What happened next was that Vicki Hester lost her nerve, and unknown to the others, slipped into a bedroom in this old house and called Chad. She located my fiancé at his father's boatyard where he was working on another sketch.

It wasn't hard to locate a hysterical girl who had been

on an island for over two hours. A month later, Dolly was institutionalized and nobody learned how she had ended up on Waties Island. Since then, Cherry Grove has built up more, and there are year-round residents, but ten years ago there was no one to hear the poor girl's cries.

Mum became the word. Besides, no one had seen any of the clique with Dolly. True, she'd hung with them, and they'd told her they were going to meet at Waties Island and would have what would be called in today's terms a "kegger." They had no idea Dolly would show up, even less of an idea that she would have the nerve to cross the fifty yards of water and come looking for them.

Chad dropped by the interrogation/ritual room to bring me a fresh cup of coffee. He asked how things were going, and I told him I was going to take on Jeremy before I saw Vicki. Chad said he'd go upstairs and see how she was doing. Last time he'd been by her room, the door had been locked and he hadn't been able to rouse her.

"Probably fell asleep from exhaustion."

"I'll check on her anyway."

I said that I was sure he would.

Chad made a face as he left the room. Still, there was a hint of a smile. In a couple of months we'd be married and we'd put all these jokers behind us.

"I want a lawyer," said Jeremy before he took a seat. He did not look at Helen McCuen in the next room.

"I think you should have one, and a very good one, too," and as I did with all the others, I read him his rights.

"I'm not going to talk to you, Chase. I have nothing to say to you."

"You don't have to. I have enough from the others to convict you for the murder of Helen McCuen."

"What—what are you talking about?"

"Jeremy, why don't you take a seat and I will lay it out for you, as will the DA for the grand jury."

"What—what'd the others say?" was all he could manage. He took a seat across from me at the table.

I leaned on the table. "Come on, Jeremy. We go back a ways. When we danced at The Attic, you tried to feel me up. You can tell me."

"Not if the way you treated me at The Attic is any indication of how you're going to treat me now."

"I'm not going to knee you in the groin to make you confess. You're on your way to prison. All that's left is to determine the number of years served."

Our former experience collector pushed away from the table and threw up his hands. "This is crazy. What reason would I have to kill Helen?"

"What reason would you have to leave Dolly Jackson on Waties Island?"

His face and his body sagged. His arms fell into his lap. "I told Helen that was nuts."

"You didn't tell her anything of the sort. You were a gleeful participant, but now, traveling with *National Geographic,* you don't need that hanging over your head. Helen was a wacko from the get-go. Now she has access to the Web, and you know a lot of National Geographic followers are Web watchers. They track people working undersea, traveling around the world, and even flying through space." I smiled again. "You just had to tie up this one loose end. That nut case on the web talking about your youthful indiscretions. And you knew she would get around to it sooner or later."

"You are cruel, Susan."

"What you did to the Jackson girl wasn't cruel?"

"It wasn't my idea."

I sat up. "What load of bull! Helen wanted a girl left on Waties Island and you were happy to accommodate. You recruited Dolly. When Vicki comes down, she's going to corroborate that Helen has been sleeping with you for years and set you on this task. Vicki didn't like sharing you with Lady Light, did she? Maybe becoming a witch would make you pay more attention to her. Or understand the spell Helen had cast over you."

"That's simply not true."

"Helen could've had anyone in your circle. Reynolds, Brandon, you, Vicki. All but Chad. That's why he was never taken into your confidence. He wouldn't do Helen's bidding. The rest of you would."

"That still doesn't make me a murderer."

"Jeremy, you've been around Helen for years. There have been numerous opportunities for you to poison her."

"Poison? What are you talking about?" His voice, however, lacked conviction.

"Remember when Vicki had the seizure after the ritual and everyone was focused on her? That's when you administered more arsenic to the slice of cake Helen ate. In the kitchen you were the one stirring the soup. There you added more poison. Enough to make her vomit up part of the contents of her stomach."

"You have no proof of this."

"Why do you think I'm talking to Vicki last? She won't know what others have said, but I know a ton. I'll get the truth out of her. It was you who suggested she play a joke on the group by pretending to have a seizure, and what could Helen do but play along. Otherwise the craft loses its allure. Besides, it was only fair. Helen was taunting everyone by bringing the group together from the Waties Island affair."

"I want an attorney."

"Jeremy, I repeat that I'm not questioning you. I'm telling you what happened and how it will play out. Helen McCuen and you were two of the cruelest bastards ever produced along the Grand Strand. Bored to death in Conway and looking for someone to toy with. You guys make that character in *An Hour To Kill* look like a piker."

Jeremy was silent for a long time. When his gaze met mine again, he said, "I haven't done any of the things you've accused me of."

"If not you, maybe Perry Jackson killed Helen. You know, the brother of the sister who was left on Waties Island."

Jeremy glanced toward the darkened hallway. "Jackson is Dolly's brother?"

"You've got it," I said with a sadistic smile.

"I didn't know."

"Neither did Helen and look at her."

He gripped the table. One quick glance in the direction of the living room corpse and he said, "Susan, you have to protect us."

"Sez who?"

"Says that badge you flashed to impress everyone."

"Maybe I identify more with the girl left on Waties Island."

"But you can't leave us at the mercy of someone like Perry Jackson." Our collector of experiences glanced around at this particular experience. He was hunched over, gripping the table, eyes darting over one shoulder, then the other. "We could all be dead once the storm passes through."

"Which was the plan all the time."

"What do you mean?"

Jeremy didn't get the chance to answer. Chad was

at the door. Gasping, brown hair down across his forehead, he grabbed the jamb to keep himself on his feet. "I found the screwdriver." In his hands was the Phillips.

"Er—where?" I asked, having a hard time pulling my attention away from what appeared to be blood on the screwdriver.

Close to tears, Chad said, "Oh, God, Susan. It was stuck in Vicki's chest."

Chapter 11

C had and I rushed upstairs. Brandon, Reynolds, and Sarge heard us coming and stuck their heads out of their rooms, each demanding to know what the hell was going on.

The door to Vicki's room was open. Chad and others tried to get around me, but I held them back. "No. This is another crime scene."

"Well," said Reynolds, "it doesn't appear you're doing very well solving mysteries."

"You don't think so?" I turned on him. "I figured out who killed Helen."

"Who?" asked several voices.

I noticed Jeremy had not followed us upstairs. I waved them away. "Stay out of here. I want to examine the body." Facing Chad, I said, "The screwdriver, please."

"Susan, you don't think . . . ."

"Chad, I've told you before. I don't think. I investigate. That's what I'm paid to do." I took the screwdriver and stuck it in the pocket of my jeans. "Why were you in her room?"

"The door opened when I tried it."

"Why did you try it?"

"I couldn't get Vicki to answer."

I looked at the other young men. "Did any of you hear Chad calling to Vicki?"

They all shook their heads, and Sarge asked, "In this weather?"

I left them, closing the door behind me and leaning against it to catch my breath and collect my thoughts. After seeing Jeremy pull the screwdriver from Helen's chest, why had Chad done the same stupid thing?

"And get back into your rooms," I ordered by raising my voice and coming off the door. I kept my hand off the doorknob area. Fingerprints, you know. Or the fact that I was trembling. My fiancé was setting himself up for a fall, and the damn naïve guy that he was couldn't see the train wreck ahead.

A great deal of mumbling could be heard over the whistling of the storm, the splattering of the rain, and the groaning of a house that might lie in the center of the storm's path. However, that wasn't my immediate concern.

Vicki Hester lay on her back across the bed, a pool of blood on her blouse. She had not otherwise been injured, though there were handprints of blood alongside her body and a place in the bedcovers where someone's haunches had rumpled the bedcover. Chad had sat there, the killer, too.

I walked around the room, first making sure there was nothing I might disturb on the floor. No sign of a struggle, only blood on Vicki's hand where she had probably gripped the screwdriver before dying.

Vicki had clothes in the closet, as if she'd been here for a while or was planning a long visit.

Why not? From what I had gleaned from the interviews, this house was a meeting place for this group. First thing I was going to do when the hurricane passed over was check the ownership and rental records. And learn what Helen McCuen had said to Wendy Archibald to get her to vamoose.

If I survived the storm. Just because you were lucky with Hugo, what makes you think you can do it twice?

On top of the dresser lay the usual paraphernalia a woman would use to fix her hair and face, sorted in colorful plastic bags so they could be taken down the hall to the bathroom. No dresser drawers were pulled out. The room was lit by a light on the bedside table: Chad's oversized flash, which gave off enough light to illuminate even the corners.

The bed was made, the face of the electric clock blank. A few nighttime items, such as lip balm and a water bottle, occupied the nightstand. I was tempted to open and smell or taste it, but with the hole in the girl's chest, I figured there was little reason. Leave that to the crime scene techs—if this house was still standing when Jacqueline and her CSI techs got the chance to investigate.

I returned to the bed. The dead woman's eyes were closed, probably by Chad. I put fingers to her neck to see if there was a possible pulse.

None, and the body still warm.

As I stood over the bed, I realized there was a door that led to the adjoining room. Reaching around the old-fashioned doorknob to avoid smearing any prints, I twisted the stem where it joined the door. The knob turned but the door would not open.

Suddenly, the knob was jerked from my hand, the door opened, and Reynolds Pearce stood there. "What now?"

"You had access to the women's room?"

"Of course not. The door's locked on their side. What do you think I am, some kind of a pervert?"

That didn't seem to require an answer.

He glanced at the girl on the bed and shuddered. "Susan, I didn't do this."

"Reynolds, try to remain calm."

He continued to tremble. "Someone doesn't want us to leave this house alive."

"And who would that be?"

"Chad."

"Why Chad?"

"He let us know how ticked off he was when we were on the porch."

"About how you played him about Jackson's sister?"

"Yeah," he said rather reluctantly.

"Reynolds, I can't see my fiancé throwing away his future over your sorry past."

"What about Sarge? He wants to see us dead. And he has good reason."

"Reynolds, why don't you lie down for a while?"

"I'm going, I'm going."

Except, I thought as I closed the door and locked it, if I were Perry Jackson, my first two victims would've been male, figuring I could handle the women, or at least cow them. Then again, Helen McCuen might have been a target of opportunity.

Or the example of what was to come.

Sitting on the sofa in the living room, vomiting and helpless as she sat there, it would've been easy for Sarge to slam the Phillips screwdriver home and walk out of the living room and onto the porch.

But Vicki Hester hadn't been poisoned. From the blow to her chest, she'd taken a pounding from the same screwdriver. Someone wanted to make sure she died, and very quickly. Not a sound uttered or a chance for a scream. Not that you were likely to hear what was happening with the rain and the wind. Now the wind was from the north. What was up with this storm?

I returned to the adjoining door and muttered a curse. Reynolds had gotten under my skin about Chad, and I'd forgotten to ask the obvious question. I rapped on the door, down low, where there might not be any prints.

"Yes?" It sounded as if he got off his bed and stumbled over to the door.

"Reynolds, did you hear anything from your side of the door."

"In this storm? Of course not."

Reynolds was right. There was entirely too much wind and rain to hear anything that might've happened in the adjoining room. Still, it's the law enforcement officers that get to ask all the dumb little questions.

I returned to the bed, and using the rubber gloves I had in my jeans' pocket, turned Vicki's head one way, then the other. I pulled open her blouse by forcing the buttons from behind the slit, still hoping there might be fingerprints somewhere.

Yeah. Prints that might exonerate your stupid fiancé for pulling the screwdriver from the girl's chest.

A small hole in the chest over the left breast drew my attention, and raising Vicki up by the shoulders—where I saw no signs of a struggle—I saw where the screwdriver had driven through and out her back, puncturing the back of the blouse.

For the first time I realized someone would have to inform Helen's parents. I had only a casual history with the others, but I'd have to be the one to break the news. I owed the McCuens that much. I straightened up.

Stupid girl! You had it all and threw it away.

Unproductive thoughts.

I returned my attention to the dead girl with her pale complexion and tangle of brown hair. Now Vicki would be the center of attention for her family. The child who did not make it.

I bit my lip. There were no defensive marks. Vicki, like Helen, had trusted her attacker. Perhaps he'd been consoling her, trying to calm her. Vicki had not been putting on an act about being terrified to remain in this house. The killer must have sat on the edge of the bed, spoken reassuringly, then pulled out the Phillips and driven it into her chest.

But who?

Unfortunately, the description fitted Chad to a "T."

Jeremy had been with me for about fifteen minutes, but that meant nothing. The others said they'd been in their rooms, and that meant nothing either. Only Chad had been roaming the house, basically holing up in the kitchen.

Sarge could've come to her door and said everyone was meeting downstairs. Perry Jackson carried an air of authority, and was supposedly in charge of security. Still, there would be the risk Vicki might go through the adjoining door and exit with Reynolds Pearce, taking her chances with the devil she knew versus the one she did not know.

Or was Reynolds the monster I'd felt he was when I'd interrogated him downstairs?

Yes, Susan, line up as many suspects as you can— between your fiancé and the mounting death toll. As any defense attorney would point out, Chad, too, had walked down that downstairs hallway, past the room where Helen sat, and onto the porch to give the other guests a severe tongue-lashing.

"Susan," called Chad from the hall. His voice sounded nervous.

"Come in."

He did.

"Don't touch the doorknob on this side," I warned him as he opened the door.

His hand jerked from the door, then he stood, slack-jawed, staring at his friend. There were tears in his eyes. "I warned her . . . ."

"About what?"

Weakly, Chad brought up his arm and gestured toward the empty hallway behind him. "About the people she hung with. Every time I jumpstarted her car, I chewed her butt about hanging with Helen and Jeremy."

"Not Brandon."

"Brandon's a loser."

"And Vicki never listened to you?"

Chad shook his head and glanced around. After swallowing, he looked up. "Suze, I want out of here."

I took his hands. There was blood from the screwdriver and it would match the fluid from Vicki Hester's chest. I said, "If it wasn't for the storm, we'd be gone."

Now his arms encircled me. "I'm so sorry I brought you here."

"You had to make these people look you in the eye. And you had to look them in the eye when you accused them of that horrible thing they had done over ten years ago, and how they had made you a party to the whole scene."

An arm released me to wipe across his eyes. "But why'd I allow you to come along? It's so stupid. I brought you into the path of more than a hurricane."

"Like I said: Where you go, I go."

He shrugged out of my embrace. "It was a damn dumb thing to do."

"Agreed, but if the killer hoped the storm would remove any trace of murder, your bringing me along certainly bitched up things for him."

"God, but that's looking on the bright side."

"When I'm with you that's the only side there is."

He took my hands. "Can you ever forgive me?"

"I already have. That's what marriage is all about."

He looked over my shoulder at his dead friend. "If I'd only pressed Vicki."

"You didn't want to shatter her. You knew she was fragile and needy."

"I sure didn't want to be needed by Helen McCuen, but she was always there, pressing me."

"To go all the way."

"Or smoking dope or join a crowd going into the woods and getting loaded. It made me suspicious."

"Of what?"

"That she wanted to see me in the hallway at school and smirk."

"She did anyway. After you turned her down."

"Yes," he had to agree. "Helen always had to be top dog. You really think she was poisoned?"

"Yes."

"But how? We ate the same food and no one's come down with anything."

"She was poisoned by someone close to her, and they took a very long time doing it."

"That lets Sarge off the hook."

"Actually, you could make a decent case for Helen's having committed suicide."

Startled, he said, "How's that?"

"Not only did she know Perry Jackson shared the same surname with Dolly, she invited everyone who participated in the Waties Island affair, and while no one in their right mind thought she could pull off halting a hurricane, everyone came. Helen had to be slightly wacko to take such a chance. That's what I mean about making a case for suicide."

"So she conned me again."

"Why wouldn't you want to strut your stuff? You build some of the most beautiful boats along the Grand Strand. Helen was a witch, and Jeremy was lucky to still have his off-and-on job as a photographer with *National Geographic*."

I stopped.

"What is it?"

I snapped my fingers. "What was bothering me about Jeremy. He works for *National Geographic*, but he's brought no cameras to a hurricane party."

"That is odd, isn't it?"

"Think he's using videotape?"

"You mean, like spying on us?"

"Could be." I was thinking hard.

"Then he might have scenes of the murder."

"It's something I should talk to him about."

"I'll go with you."

"Stay here. I don't want anyone disturbing Vicki." Glancing at the body, I added, "And don't touch her. Don't touch a thing, Chad."

He nodded, staring at the dead woman.

I started away, but he called out to me. "Suze, I'm sorry I picked up the screwdriver."

I smiled reassuringly from the hallway. "You didn't want her to be hurt. You wanted to help her again."

"You have to believe there was never anything between us."

"Sure," I said with a grin, "but I have to keep my main man on his toes."

Chad smiled as I continued down the hall and rapped on Jeremy's door.

Reynolds Pearce, who had said he could hear little in this storm, opened his door. "Jeremy's not been there since he went downstairs to be interviewed by you."

I found Jeremy in the ritual room. He was in the process of climbing down a short stepladder in the far corner. He held a small black plastic box that had a lens mounted on it. A wireless video camera.

"I'm going to have to confiscate that video cam and I'll need to know where the others are. And how many."

"Screw you, too, Chase."

"You don't want a lawyer present?" I asked, setting myself by spreading my feet.

"I don't need a lawyer to deal with you."

"What about the accusations of poisoning your dear friend, Helen McCuen."

"I didn't."

"Jeremy, when this storm is over, Jacqueline Marion and her techs are going to swarm all over this house and they are going to be looking for the arsenic or whatever was used to kill Helen. And some of that arsenic will be found on someone's clothing."

"What reason would I have had to kill Helen?"

"Besides proving she still held sway over the clique, even in the face of a hurricane, she had invited Chad. That made the situation even dicier. Chad's just the sort to go to the authorities and fall on his sword."

"Then that makes everyone a suspect."

"Come on, Jeremy, you've been handling Helen's food for years. That would amuse you, wouldn't it, that Helen thought she was the queen bee, and all the time you held her life in your hands. Where are the other video cams?"

"Two outside. Under the gables. Probably useless." He pointed behind me. "The other's overhead in the shadows of the corner. It's motion activated."

When I turned to see the other camera, Jeremy hit me very hard and very quickly on the jaw.

Chapter 12

C had held up my head and told me not to move. My hand came up to where my chin hurt. The right side of my face ached. I tried to remember what had happened. The darkness disappeared when a light moved. That didn't make any sense. Lights didn't move.

It was a flashlight in a darkened room. Weird shadows bounced off a wall when Chad tried to comfort me and still hold his light. But where was I?

I saw a couple of chairs and table. No overhead lights. This room and the adjoining one were lit by candles and someone appeared to be sitting on the couch.

Lit by candles?

What the hell happened? I don't usually get poked on the jaw when Chad and I are burning candles.

He had the same question. "What happened?"

I didn't remember.

"You came down here to talk to Jeremy about his video cameras. Is he the one who did this?"

My eyes squinted and I felt tears. My jaw ached, but I could wiggle my toes and flex my hands.

Then I remembered Jeremy had hit me. The bastard!

"Could I . . ." I started. "Could I have some ice?"

"I'm sure there's still some in the cooler." Chad placed my head down gently. "You stay right here."

"And find a cloth to wrap it in."

At the door, he turned and faced me. "You just stay where you are, Susan. I'll handle Jeremy."

"Get the ice first . . . and the cloth."

Once he was gone, I rolled over on my chest, then got to my hands and knees. Jeez, but my jaw hurt. I saw a short stepladder, like something used in a kitchen. Two blue steps made of plastic. I used it to stagger to my feet.

Now I could remember who sat in the living room.

The dead Helen McCuen.

The whole scene was macabre. I'd have to throw a sheet over her. But that would have to wait until later.

My next step took me to the jamb of the pocket door, where I held on tight. I was a little bit dizzy.

Clutching the wall, I was able to stumble down the hallway. Crossing the hall to the spiral stairs posed a major problem, so I simply lunged, caught the railing, and held on to the post as I slid to the floor. Tears ran down my cheeks. My jaw hurt like hell.

Raising up, gasping for breath, and wiping away tears, I stared at Helen in the living room. Considering the alternative, I was in great shape.

I turned and started up the stairs, but my legs needed convincing. To initiate movement, I grasped the railing and hauled myself to my feet. Chad would be along any moment and he had to find me upstairs—not lying across the steps.

I could barely hear the wind and rain over the trudging as my feet slammed into each step. One slow step at a time, and using the railing, I pulled myself up the staircase that wrapped around the interior wall of the house.

Made the first landing, then took a breather. Had to. Sweat broke out all over.

It was Chad's voice that got me moving up the longer staircase, the one clinging to the wall.

"Suze? Where are you?" His voice sounded like he was in the ritual room.

No answer necessary. Once he reached the bottom of the stairs, he, too, would hear my trudging onward and upward.

Still, my legs felt weak. I didn't know how much longer I could stand. Stumbling forward, I made the next landing. Just a few more steps and I'd be across from Jeremy's door at the head of the stairs.

The door was closed. The damn thing would be locked if the bastard knew what was good for him.

At the bottom of the stairs, Chad looked up. "Susan, what the hell are you doing?" In his hand was a kitchen towel bulging with what I could only hope was ice.

I would need that. Later. "I'm going to pay a visit . . . to Jeremy Knapp."

Chad came up the stairs after me. "You do and he could kill you this time."

I continued pulling myself up the four or five steps to the second floor. "I want to know why . . . he didn't kill me . . . when he had the opportunity."

Chad made the turn on the first landing as I finished the stairs. There I clung to the railing, swaying back and forth, almost tumbling backwards and down all those stairs I'd recently conquered.

To my left was the cot where Sarge bunked. It was empty. Sarge was supposed to be down the hall in Chad's and my room. Something twitched in my mind about that.

"Susan, for God's sake!" Ice clattered on the stairs as Chad raced for me.

Before he could reach me, I threw myself at the door, turning my side so I wouldn't hit face first.

The door did not give, but my body did, and I collapsed in front of it. Voices sounded down the hall. Sarge and Reynolds Pearce. They wanted to know what the hell was going on once again.

As Chad knelt beside me, I summoned up enough energy to slam my fist against the bottom of the door. "Come out of there . . . Jeremy."

Good chance he might not hear me with the storm and the shouting as Sarge lumbered down the hall. Or Chad's voice in my ear, asking if I was nuts.

No. Just pissed off.

Chad picked me up and held me in his arms. That felt good. Now if the pain in my face and shoulder would go away. The storm, too, for good measure.

From inside his room, Jeremy called out, "Get away from me, Chase!"

As Sarge bent over me, he appeared puzzled—from what I could make out through my tear-filled eyes. I used a hand to wipe the tears away.

Chad explained. "Jeremy hit Susan when she was asking for his video cameras."

"Video cameras?" asked Reynolds.

I have to give Sarge his due. The former sergeant kept his eye on the ball. He reached over me and hammered on the door. "Come out of there, Knapp. You can't hit a woman and get away with it."

Well, maybe he was overstepping his bounds. "Sarge . . ." I started.

"Miss Chase, you stay out of this."

"I'll wait out the storm in here," shouted Jeremy. "I don't want anything to do with any of you. You can try to get in, but I have furniture piled against the door. And it's locked," he added, unnecessarily.

"You'd better come out, Jeremy."

"Why? I'm safer in here, and besides, these are my videotapes and your fiancée thinks I killed Helen. She probably thinks I killed Vicki, too. I didn't kill anyone."

Everyone looked at me.

"I think it was the cameras . . . that set him off," I could finally say. Tears continued down my cheeks and I wiped them away.

"What cameras?" asked Reynolds again.

"He filmed the ritual room and the storm outside," explained my fiancé.

"And what else?" asked Reynolds, chewing his lower lip. "Did he have cameras in our rooms?"

"We don't know."

Sarge slammed his fist against the door again. "We'll want to see those videotapes, Knapp."

"You'll get nothing. These tapes are the property of the *National Geographic.*"

"You don't work for *National Geographic*—"

Chad cut him off. "Jeremy, local law enforcement will want to see those tapes."

"There's nothing on them but the ritual and the storm. That's all. You have to believe me."

"Well," Sarge said, appraising the door, "he's got a point. We don't need him."

"And we don't want him around if he killed Helen and Vicki." Reynolds glanced over his shoulder. "Staying in our rooms sounds like a very good idea."

Chad looked down the hall in the direction of the room next to Jeremy's and across from Reynolds's. "Where's Brandon?"

"In his room, if he has any sense," Reynolds said.

Sarge stepped down the hall a few feet, flashlight in hand, and tried Brandon's door.

There were five rooms, three on the left, two on the right, which was followed by the bathroom. The women had shared one bedroom, the men bunked alone.

Chad helped me to my feet and—when I insisted—down to Brandon's room. Reynolds tried to follow me, but I ordered him to stand guard at Jeremy's door.

"I want to know if he comes out."

"While you're watching," Chad said, "go downstairs and pick up the ice and the cloth I dropped."

I clarified that. "Go down and pick up the ice as you come back up. That way you'll be able to watch the door and see if Jeremy leaves his room."

Reynolds glanced at the door, then disappeared around the corner.

"Sweet angel of mercy," exclaimed Sarge before we reached Brandon's bedroom door.

In the light from Chad's lantern, we could see a long, slim figure hanging from a ceiling fixture that was a combination heavy-duty fan support and lamps with old-timey glass shades.

Sarge had his arms around the torso and under the arms. "Help me here!" he shouted.

"Untie him from the lamp," I ordered from the door. "But leave the rope around his neck."

The men looked at me but did as I ordered. I leaned against the door as they lowered the body to the woven rug. Without Chad's and Sarge's lights the room would've been in darkness but for a flashlight on the nightstand, glowing feebly, its batteries going.

The rope around our former vampire was thin, white nylon, and tied firmly around his neck. Both men knelt beside the body.

"He's dead, Suze."

As I slumped in the hallway door, who should appear but Jeremy Knapp.

Looking up at him, I said, "Come down here, Jeremy. I want to kick your butt."

He handed four videocassettes to me as Reynolds appeared in the doorway with the fabric bag of ice.

"My God!" exclaimed our investment banker when Jeremy straightened up after blocking Reynolds' view. The towel fell to the floor, scattering ice.

"I'm sorry I hit you, Susan, but you have no right . . ." Jeremy's voice trailed off as he, too, noticed the body on the rug. "Mother Mary of God. He really did it."

"Did what?" I was crawling around scooping up ice and socking it away in the kitchen towel.

As Jeremy gaped at the dead man, Chad crossed the room in two quick steps, and threw a punch that knocked our experience collector out of the room and across the hall. As he passed, Chad's leg knocked the towel and ice from my hand, scattering ice everywhere.

"A little help here, Sarge."

As Perry turned, he saw Chad pull Jeremy to his feet as if to punch him again. The former sergeant scrambled to his feet, crossed the room, and entered the hall. Stepping on the cubes of ice, his feet went out from under him, and he finished crossing the hall by landing on his butt and thrusting his feet ahead of him.

Which was enough to save Jeremy from a further beating. One of Sarge's boots landed on the back of Chad's leg and all three men went down in a pile. I ignored them and crawled into Brandon's room. From my pocket I pulled a flashlight and began to examine the body.

For the first time, Brandon wore no hat, and his white

throat revealed a horizontal furrow cut by the nylon. The ligature ran just below the dead man's Adam's apple and was about the same size as the rope. There appeared to be bruising above the rope, and when I moved the light across his face, I saw pinhead-sized red dots, or minute hemorrhages.

Brandon Calhoun had not killed himself.

I became aware of order being reestablished in the hallway, and that I could hear the rain and the wind outside. That's what you always heard—if you weren't getting hell beat out of you or your boyfriend wasn't beating hell out of Jeremy Knapp.

I heard Sarge shout, "That's not going to do your girlfriend any good."

"It'll do me plenty," Chad said, probably wrestling to get away from Sarge.

"Stay away from me," moaned Jeremy. "I've already apologized."

"You hit Susan and you think this ends it? I'll damn well kill you."

Jeez. I didn't need to hear that. I crawled over to the bed and propped myself up. I glanced at the overturned chair across the room. I could imagine Sarge had kicked it out of the way before we entered the room so he could get under Brandon and lift him up—if his intent had been to save our former vampire from strangulation.

Chad walked in the room, rubbing his knuckles. "I'll finish the SOB before the storm's over."

From where I sat alongside the latest corpse, I asked, "Do you really want to say something like that in front of a law enforcement officer?"

"Suze, this is Chad."

"I know who you are, and by your comment I can tell you've already relegated me to the kitchen, barefoot and pregnant."

"I don't know what you're talking about."

"I could've handled Jeremy Knapp."

"Susan, you truly are nuts. You were lying on the floor when I found you—both times—in the ritual room and at the head of the stairs. You weren't going to clean anyone's clock. That was my job, and I plan on finishing it."

"Chad, I can defend myself. He sucker-punched me."

"I won't discuss this. We'll just have to agree to disagree." There was no smile when he added, "And I'll make damn sure I watch what you teach our daughters."

The other three men entered the room. Jeremy held the ice-filled kitchen cloth to his nose. Blood ran down his neck and onto his short-sleeved shirt.

Well, score one for the home team.

Sarge stared at the dead Brandon Calhoun. "I wasn't soon enough."

"Nobody was soon enough," I said, feeling very, very tired. "Brandon was strangled, then strung up to make it look like a suicide."

"What?" said several at the same time.

"You know this for a fact?" asked one, and "How do you know?" came the chorus.

"Chad, would you give me a hand?"

My fiancé pulled me to my feet and said, "You never got the ice."

I touched my face. It still hurt. "You'll just have to hope the swelling goes down before the wedding." The smile I tried, faltered. When Sarge reached for the dead man's neck, I said, "Perry, don't do that. Have everyone removed from the scene, lock the door, and give me the key."

"There are keys?" asked Reynolds.

"I have one," said the former sergeant, straightening up. "Well, I did have one. A master key is in the kitchen in one of the drawers."

"Not at the rate we're finding bodies in this house," I said. "I want all of you to raise your hands over your heads, spread your feet, and let me search you."

"What?" asked Reynolds.

"I want to see if that key is on anyone."

"What about you?" asked Jeremy. Speaking through an ice compress made his voice sound funny.

"The lady's right." The former sergeant stood with his back to me, raised his hands, and let me run my hands over his body. I found a set of keys.

"To the APC, car, and my apartment," he explained, and that's just what they appeared to be, though the one to the APC was nothing more than a padlock key, nothing like the skeleton key used to lock any doors in this old house.

"Perry," I said, returning the keys, "even if you were to reach your vehicle, the storm surge would have already buried it under several feet of water."

"I don't think so. It's blocks away. Lady Light didn't want a military vehicle around her ritual."

"And how were you going to negotiate the distance between here and there? No, you're stuck with us."

He considered the thought. "Then search them. Strip search them if you have to." Sarge noticed the reluctance of one Jeremy Knapp. "I'll go find some tissues to stuff in Mr. Knapp's nose. If we're stuck here, we might need his help."

"God, but I hope not," said my fiancé, glowering at Jeremy.

Sarge disappeared out the door.

Next up was Reynolds, who stood still as I patted him down. "My personal keys are in my room. If you want to see them."

Then Jeremy. He had no keys and the same excuse. "In my room," he said through his nose.

After searching my fiancé's pockets, I had no reason to continue to look. I found the missing master in his back pocket, the one where he didn't keep his wallet.

Chad's eyes widened. "Where did that come from?"

I dropped the key into the pocket of my jeans.

Reynolds gaped, but Jeremy beamed. "Looks like you've found your killer, Susan, and I'd like to be the first to congratulate you."

In one quick step I was across the room slapping the smirk off his face. Ice went flying again, bouncing off Sarge's broad chest as he came through the door.

"What's this?" he asked.

Reynolds identified the killer as my fiancé, adding, "Susan found the key on Chad."

Sarge looked puzzled. "But why?"

"That's just what I was wondering." Looking around the room, I said, "Someone planted this on Chad. He didn't have any reason to murder anyone."

"Susan, you can't have it both ways," Reynolds said.

"Yeah," chimed in Jeremy, his voice muffled as he stuffed tissue paper in his nose. "You think everyone's a suspect but your fiancé."

"And Chad's motive would be?"

"You seem to come up with reasons why the rest of us are guilty. Don't you think you could do the same for him?"

"Suze, you can't honestly believe I had anything to do with this."

I said nothing.

Jeremy snapped his fingers and spoke through his nose again. "I've got it. Chad wants us all dead because it's the only thing that will soothe his conscience about his participation at Waties Island."

Sarge looked from Jeremy to my fiancé. "Would that be correct, Mr. Rivers?"

"All I know is that Vicki called and told me a girl was stuck on Waties Island. Said she'd be at the Cherry Grove Landing when I arrived. I got there as fast as I could."

"Why didn't you call EMS?"

"I didn't trust them to find Waties Island."

"But if they were in the area, they had to know where the island was and its condition at high tide."

"Sergeant, you don't know how things work along the Grand Strand. The EMS personnel are first-rate, but people come from all over to take those jobs because they want to live at the beach. That doesn't mean they'll know where to look or how to get there."

"You've got to be kidding."

"This was over ten years ago. It was a different Grand Strand then."

"And," I said rather softly, "you've taken girls out there, haven't you, Chad?"

"Yes." He stared at the floor. "Before the causeway was built."

"So you'd be trapped on the island and have to spend the night together."

He looked up. "Sometimes we do things we aren't very proud of. Lots of boys have taken girls out to Waties Island for the same purpose. It's much safer than parking on deserted roads." Chad regarded the former military type. "Something I'm sure you're familiar with."

Sarge nodded. "It's a game all people play—"

"All boys play," I injected.

The four boys looked at me, but I spoke to Chad.

"And if you made this incident public, it would get your friends in trouble."

Chad shook his head. "Not true. No matter what anyone thinks, none of these people were my friends." To Perry Jackson, he said, "Sergeant Jackson, I had your sister at the hospital less than forty-five minutes after I received the call. You can believe that or not."

Jackson merely nodded.

"Then you went looking for Vicki?"

"I tried, but this was before everyone carried a cell phone. And it was Friday night. She wasn't at home." He glanced at Sarge again. "I know that for a fact. I didn't connect with Vicki until Monday at school. I work in my father's boatyard Saturdays and sketch my vessels on Sundays." He glanced at me. "As Susan often says, I have my head in the clouds when it comes to my boats."

"What was Miss Hester's explanation?" asked Sarge.

"Oh, she was good. Very good. Vicki looked me up between classes. We didn't share classes and Vicki always lunched off school grounds."

"What did she tell you?" I asked.

"That she thought I was going to meet her at one landing and I left from another."

"She was lying."

"I didn't know that at the time." Looking at Dolly's brother, Chad said, "All I had on my mind was getting your sister to the hospital."

"When did you figure Perry and Dolly were related?" I asked.

"Not right away, but since everyone else was here and Dolly and Perry share the same last name . . . ." Chad lowered his eyes. "I kept meaning to go by the hospital, but when I finally did, Dolly had already been sent to Bull Street." Where, at the time, the seriously deranged were stashed in the state capital.

I took Chad's arm and squeezed it. "And it would never dawn on you that Vicki Hester would be a party to such a perverse stunt."

"You're damn right," he said, looking every man in the eye. "I didn't have contact with any of these jokers. But I knew Vicki hung with them."

"I believe that's what she counted on, that you'd simply pull the Jackson girl off the island and accept her explanation. But the moment Vicki showed with those groceries, you knew what was up."

Chad nodded.

"Let me guess," I said. "Vicki Hester's car didn't break down the rest of the school year."

Chad tried to remember. "That was more than ten years ago, but you could be right."

"Of course it didn't break down. Vicki had been warned by Jeremy to stay away from you."

Everyone looked at our video taper.

Jeremy shook his head and denied everything.

"If you think about it," I continued, "you'll realize you didn't see much of Vicki the rest of the semester."

"I can't be sure. My first boat was in production. I was pretty much living at the plant, and making up excuses why I shouldn't have to attend college."

"I've been there," I said with a smile. "Sometimes it's hard to get you away from the drafting table. I'm thinking of not allowing one in the house."

"If we ever see that house." He looked from Reynolds to Jeremy to Sarge. "One of these three is a killer, and he doesn't plan to let any of us get on with our lives."

Chapter 13

"**W**ell, I can tell you for sure that I'm no killer." Reynolds glanced at the rest of us in Brandon's bedroom. "But I think it's best we all adjourn to the living room or kitchen where we can keep an eye on each other."

"The kitchen," seconded Sarge, "not the living room."

"I'll go along with that," came a nasal voice. "It's time Susan learned I had nothing to do with these deaths."

"Well," Sarge said, "one thing's for sure, whether the killer plans on killing more of us, for sure he won't want to be here when the storm's over and the National Guard arrives. I imagine they're already massing down the road and making plans to move in as soon as the governor orders them."

"That's right," said Chad, putting an arm around me. "And if we have to separate, you guys will just have to find someone to trust. I'm already buddied up."

"Then I would suggest," said Jeremy with a sly smile, "that Susan watch her backside."

Chad's arm dropped off me as he moved toward

Jeremy. "Want me to finish what I started in the hall?" he asked.

Sarge stepped between them. "Now, now, you can settle this after the storm."

"If anyone survives," I couldn't help but throw in.

"It would be more productive," suggested Reynolds, "if we all went downstairs and had something to eat. The kitchen's just the place for that, but first we throw a sheet over Helen."

"And tell ghost stories," said Jeremy with a muffled laugh. "I'll lead the way. I've got to have more ice for my nose."

"How about offering Susan the first cubes," said Chad. "She earned them when you popped her in the face."

"Look," said Jeremy, stopping at Brandon's door, "I'm sorry for what I did, but you have to understand—Susan accused me of murder. And she wanted to take my disks." He glanced at the disks on the nightstand where I had put them. "Well, there they are and they're all yours."

"I'll never forget what you did," said Chad, picking up the disks.

"Yeah, Knapp," the Sarge chimed in. "You hit a woman. If anyone is the killer, I'll put my money on you."

"Oh, is that right? You're the one who has the most to gain by killing all of us. Your sister was left on that island."

"I would hope that I have a bit more self-control than some of the other people in this house."

"Don't take that tone with me," said Reynolds, delaying his exit from the room. "I know where you came from, what you are, and, if you get out of this house alive, where you're headed. You'll be a security guard the rest of your life. All of us have decent lives but—"

"That doesn't mean you're decent people."

"Jackson," interrupted Reynolds, "talk all you want. Make up all the theories about why you should do what you think you should do, but like it or not, if you don't kill us, when the storm passes, you're returning to security work while I'm returning to investment banking. I'm simply not impressed with anything you have to say."

Sarge grinned. "But you *are* afraid of me."

Reynolds stepped back, almost on top of our experience collector. "You've got that right. I agree with Jeremy that you came to this party to kill everyone. Once you arrived, however, you learned you'd have to also kill Chad Rivers and his fiancée. Now you learn Chad went to the island instead of calling EMS, and with your narrow way of thinking, perhaps that's enough reason to justify killing him. But how are you going to justify killing Susan?"

"Er—can we change the subject?" I asked.

Jeremy out and out laughed. Chad smiled and eventually so did the rest of us. After I asked Chad to bring along a sheet from Brandon's bed, we trooped out of the dead man's room, being very careful to avoid the melting ice on the stairs and hallway floor.

The head of the front stairs was dark and eerie until our lights hit it. Sarge's cot sat in darkness and a single candle burned in Jeremy's room.

"Put out that light," ordered Sarge.

Jeremy left us to do so.

At the head of the stairs, Reynolds stepped aside. "After you, Sergeant," he said, gesturing with his hand at the descending staircase.

Jackson smiled and started down the stairs, and I noticed he kept one hand on the railing at all times. At each of the two landings, he glanced back to see who might be following him. That would be me.

At the ground floor, Chad headed for the living room to cover Helen with the sheet, and he was the first to realize the body was missing.

"What this?" demanded Sarge, following my fiancé into the room. "Where's the body?" He faced us. "Where's Lady Light?"

"Damn," said Reynolds, leaning into the jamb of the pocket door. "There's someone else in the house."

We looked at him.

"Was she really dead?" Sarge directed his question to me. "Could you possibly have been mistaken?"

"What are you saying?" asked Jeremy, the final person to step off the stairs. "That witches can return from the dead?"

"There's someone else in the house," repeated Reynolds in a voice you could barely hear over the storm outside. "It's the only answer."

"Chad, please check on Vicki."

He did and Sarge went with him.

Moments later, they returned to find the rest of us waiting near the bottom of the staircase.

Chad hustled down the stairs. "She's not there either, Suze."

"I'm not surprised."

"And why is that?" asked Jeremy, in a nasal tone.

"Because someone's been playing mind games with us ever since we entered this house. This is simply another one of those games."

"But I searched the house thoroughly," protested our security guard as he finished the stairs, crossed the hallway, and joined us in the living room. "There's no one else in this house."

Reynolds had taken a seat in one of the Queen Anne

chairs, shoulders slumped. "You're wrong," he said, shaking his head, "totally wrong."

"I'll search the house again."

Reynolds glanced at one of the shuttered windows and listened to the ocean slosh across the porch. "Being outside is looking better and better."

"We could split up," suggested nasal Jeremy, "and conduct a room-to-room search."

"That's just what the killer wants," Reynolds said. "We must stick together."

"What do we do?" asked Chad. The disks lay on the coffee table, the sheet on the floor between the table and the red velvet sofa.

"We keep to the plan," I said. "Go to the kitchen and hang together."

"Everyone watches everyone," said Chad, nodding. "I like that."

"But who's watching the extra guest?" asked Reynolds, sitting up. "We don't even know who he or she is."

Sarge was still thinking to the point his face reflected the pain. "I just don't see how someone could have stayed hidden. I went over this house several times. I walked in on people."

We looked at him.

"I had the skeleton key. I walked in on Miss Hester when she wasn't completely dressed." He looked at Jeremy. "She was in your room, Mr. Knapp."

We all looked at Jeremy.

"So what?"

"Jeremy's right," said Reynolds from the Queen Anne. "That information is only good for past theories. It has nothing to do with our current situation. Someone else is in this house."

Chad said, "Someone who is playing mind games with us."

"And doing quite a good job," I added, studying our investment banker as he got to his feet.

Reynolds said, "Then I vote we move to the kitchen. But we can't eat anything. It could be poisoned."

"Nothing?" asked Chad. "There was plenty of food in the pantry."

"You can eat what you want," Jeremy said. "I think Reynolds is right. Let's gather up what candles we have and sit out the storm in the kitchen."

"And if the storm breaks into the lower level of the house?" I asked.

"We move as a group upstairs, even to the third floor, if necessary," came the nasal reply.

"Yeah," said Reynolds with a long sigh. "And probably right into the hands of this madman."

"I'm not sure the person who moved the bodies isn't one of us."

Everyone looked at me.

"We haven't always been together. There's been ample opportunity to move Helen. We might find her if we looked ourselves. That would go for Vicki, too."

"But what reason would one of us have for doing that?" asked Jeremy.

"What do you think, Reynolds?"

"Why are you asking me, Susan?"

"Because ever since you learned who Dolly Jackson's brother was, you're the one who's become the most vulnerable."

"I'm most vulnerable? You've been kicked around a bit yourself."

"No one's tried to kill me."

"Not yet," said Jeremy with a smile.

"Watch your tongue," Chad said.

The smile disappeared from Jeremy's face, and it pleased me no end.

"I don't follow what you're saying, Miss Chase."

"Simple, Sarge. I room with Chad. The killer has to take both of us out at the same time. You appear to be able to handle yourself, so—"

"He could also be the killer," suggested Jeremy.

"Or you, Mr. Knapp," said our security guard. "I compiled a dossier on everyone except Miss Chase. Sorry, ma'am, but that's why I didn't believe you were with SLED."

"Yes. It's hard to get past my good looks."

Nobody smiled.

"Your point, Sarge?" asked Chad.

"You're squeaky clean, Mr. Rivers. So clean I figured after you participated in the incident at Waties Island, you lost your nerve and retired to boat building."

"I can't deny that." He glanced at me. "I've heard the complaint before, except about the lack of nerve, especially when I take cigarette boats out. Then, I'm considered just plain stupid."

"But I did search this house thoroughly," said Sarge, "which only means—"

"That's like Susan defending Chad," broke in Jeremy in his nasal tone and still holding the ice pack to his face. "We'd expect you to defend your work."

"No, no, that's not what I'm saying."

"Then spit it out, Jackson."

"If you'd like, Mr. Knapp. There are reports of you abusing women in four different countries. Also, you don't work for *National Geographic*."

When Jeremy tried to interrupt, Sarge silenced him with an upraised hand. "Your relationship with Vicki Hester has always been abusive. She filed a complaint with the Horry County Police Department but later withdrew it." He turned to Reynolds. "So I agree with Miss Chase. You are the most vulnerable, Mr. Pearce."

"I'm not afraid of anyone in this house."

"Oh, but you are. You didn't save anyone's life on 9/11. Someone pulled you off the street when you froze, and the reason your firm in New York was happy to let you go was that you were expendable."

"I'm expendable? A security guard is telling me that he's more important than someone who buys and sells currency."

"You aren't a currency trader."

"What?"

"You're in bonds. The safe stuff."

"That's ridiculous." He looked around at the assembled group. "Everyone knows I buy and sell currency."

"Not in Charlotte and not New York. You don't have the nerve."

"What is your point?" asked my fiancé.

"That Miss Chase is correct. There is no one but us in this house, and not only because I thoroughly searched it, but because Mr. Pearce needs us to believe that someone else is in this house. He moved the bodies while we were in Brandon Calhoun's room."

"You idiots," said Reynolds, looking around, "you're going to get all of us killed if you listen to this man. There is someone else in this house."

Chad held up a hand, stopping him. "Then you're saying a simple search of the house will turn up—"

I said, "The hastily hidden bodies of both Vicki Hester and Helen McCuen. It was Reynolds who insisted we place a sheet over Helen, something, because of what else had occurred, we had forgotten."

"And Reynolds did this why?" asked Chad, studying the blond-headed man.

"Because he knows you and I didn't kill either woman, nor did we kill Brandon. But Reynolds knows either Jeremy or Perry did kill both women, and that he doesn't have the nerve."

"So, what you're saying is the safest course of action was for Reynolds to hide the bodies and claim there had to be someone else in the house."

I nodded in agreement. "Reynolds wants to sell us on the idea of staying together."

There was a thump on the front porch. The sound drew our attention to, not only the sound, but the wind. It was blowing from offshore again. The hurricane was coming ashore, and had possibly sent something on ahead of the storm, perhaps another palmetto tree.

"So you actually did this?" Jeremy raised a hand as if to strike Reynolds. "You took those two poor girls and stuck them in a closet somewhere."

"Jeremy," said my fiancé, "if you hit another person, I'm going to deck you."

There were several thumps at the front door.

Jeremy lowered his hand at Chad's threat, and Reynolds moved away, suddenly finding himself next to the former army sergeant. He quickly moved away.

The thumping continued at the front door.

"Could the girls be out there?" asked Jeremy.

"The girls are dead," I said.

"Another palmetto?" asked another.

We listened. Hard.

With a shrug, Jeremy said, "It's the wind."

"I think we should get back to the matter at hand," Sarge said. "What we have to decide is . . ."

The rest was lost on me as I moved toward the anteroom doors, which, of course, lead to the front double doors and the shutters beyond them. Outside, the wind howled and rain pelted the doors. Inside, my jaw still hurt. I needed some ice. Still, I thought I heard a muffled voice on the other side of the double set of doors.

Sarge followed me. "Miss Chase, it wouldn't matter if there *was* someone out there. We couldn't open the door."

"And why is that?" asked Reynolds.

"Because the storm would gain a foothold," said Jeremy, as if he were talking to a child, "possibly destroying the house."

"Why couldn't someone enter from the rear of the house? I mean, if someone is actually out there."

Jeremy reminded Reynolds of the drill-and-screw routine he and I had applied to the plywood at the back of the beach house. "You really can't go out that way."

Sarge nodded in agreement.

Me, however, I was flinging back a door of the anteroom so I could better hear what was happening on the front porch. The wind was steady now. Not the odd gusts we had heard off and on during the day, and water had puddled up between the two sets of double doors.

"Miss Chase, I can't allow you to do that." The former soldier put a hand on my shoulder.

"Sarge," I said, turning my head and looking at him over my shoulder, "do you want me to break something?"

He did not smile. He did not grin. He only stared at me in disbelief.

"Take your hand off my fiancée."

"Stay out of this, Chad." I never looked at Chad but continued to stare at the pockmarked face.

"But, Suze—"

"This is between the Sarge and me."

We never got a chance to settle the matter. Beyond the door anyone who wasn't deaf could hear the voice.

"Hey, in the house! Let me in."

I wrenched out of Sarge's grasp and put my ear against the door.

"Who is it?" I screamed.

"It's me, babe. Kenny Mashburn."

"You're right," I said, leaving the door. "There's no one out there."

Sarge watched me go while Chad approached the door. "Hey, outside!"

"Hey, yourself. Open the door. I gots to get out of this storm. It's already up to my ankles."

That just might be true. Water oozed under the door and had dampened the anteroom floor.

"What are you doing out there?" demanded Chad.

"What you mean? Trying to get out of the storm."

"Go away," ordered Sarge. "We don't have enough provisions for another party."

"Hey," said the voice from outside, "I gots enough provisions for plenty of parties."

Chad looked at me, standing down the hall away from everyone. "What does he mean, Suze?"

"Kenny Mashburn's a dope dealer. He's the one who called me on the phone during dinner."

Chad's mouth formed a small O.

"I could use a hit right about now," said Reynolds. "Let him in."

Perry Jackson crossed his arms and stood in front of the door as Kenny continued dealing something other than dope.

"Hey, don't you want to party? I mean it is a party, ain't it?"

"You got the real stuff?" shouted Reynolds, stepping as close as he felt comfortable being that near to Sarge.

"I've got what you need, man. Now open up."

I shook my head. If anyone was fool enough to open that door . . . for that fool.

Hurricane winds were generally from the direction of the storm, hence the size and the force of the surge, but there had been some odd gusts on the sides of the house. Those could have been tornadoes spawned by the hurricane. To have to deal with not only the hurricane and the killer inside the house—a tornado would have the strength to rip off the top of this house. Any house.

I shivered. Maybe my idea of eventually moving to the third floor was not such a smart one.

"Hey," came Kenny's voice from outside. "What you doing in there? Taking a vote?"

If we were, Kenny would get mine—for remaining outside. Anyone dense enough to be out in the middle of . . .

I really didn't want to go there. I was, once again, attending a hurricane party.

"Stand aside, Sarge," Chad said.

Jeremy stood shoulder to shoulder with him. "It's not right to leave someone out in the storm."

From beside them, Reynolds Pearce mumbled, "I think we should toss Susan out. After all, she's the one who killed Lady Light, and the storm has probably returned for her."

"Chad," I said from down the hall, "I don't think you'd better open that door. The wind's been acting way weird."

"Sorry, Suze, I'm not leaving anyone, including a drug dealer, outside."

Kenny put in his two cents' worth. "Hey, folks, if you don't let me inside quick my stuff's going to get wet and we ain't gonna have no party."

And with that kind of reasoning, Reynolds forgot about the hurricane to return and joined the other three at the door.

Sarge was adamant. "I'm not doing this."

Chad glanced at his support unit, standing left and right of him. "It's three to one."

"But Miss Chase is right. We can't open the door."

"Oh, then, you'd prefer I'd not gone to Waties Island and brought your sister ashore?"

Jackson thought for a moment, and then nodded, turned around, and gripped the lock, turning it. He opened the door.

The wind threw the door back in his face, and, as large as he was, Perry Jackson was thrown against the narrow wall of the vestibule. Chad and Jeremy fell back against the unopened second door, and something yellow slithered inside the house between everyone's legs, then into the hall.

When Chad reached to slam the door shut, the wind grabbed him and sucked him outside. He became twisted around, facing us, with only his hands on the edge of the closed outer door; legs extended as the wind pulled him into the storm.

I rushed forward, but before I could get to him, Jeremy had Chad's arms and was pulling him back inside. Still, the wind was too much for him. Even for Perry Jackson, who had his hand on the back of Jeremy's belt, the other hand on one of the closed interior doors. All three men were sucked out and tumbled across the porch. When the wind reversed itself again, only two of them fell back into the anteroom and the safety of the house.

Chapter 14

Running for the front door, I tripped over Kenny Mashburn and fell on top of him. The young black man wore a yellow slicker head to toe. His boots dripped water. By now, all of us were soaked and the floor, too. Wind blew rain into the house by the bucketfuls.

"Hey, babe," said the sleazeball, looking up at me, "I knew you couldn't resist me."

"Get away from me, you bastard!" I fought my way free and back to my feet. "I have to get Chad back inside."

"He that white boy—"

"Who was dumb enough to let some scumbag in here."

"Hey," said Kenny, standing up and dripping water, "let's not be calling people names. The hurricane's coming ashore and now's not a time to be picky about your friends."

"I'm always picky about my friends," I said, heading toward the door.

It did no good. I couldn't open the door against the pressure of the storm, and before it could reverse itself again, Sarge and Jeremy forcibly removed me from the anteroom with me screaming Chad's name. The shutters were locked, the exterior door, and then the anteroom.

"We've got to open the door! Chad's out there!"

"No, we don't," said Jeremy. "I saw him washed down the steps and out to sea. He's gone."

I fought to get free, flailing around with my hands and fists. "Like I'd . . . take your word . . . ." I broke free and made for the door again.

"No," Sarge said, grabbing me around the waist and holding me back, "we are not going to do that again." He glanced at Jeremy. "Mr. Knapp is correct in his assessment. Your fiancé was washed out to sea."

From the living room, Reynolds Pearce said, "He knew the risk."

"That's right," Jeremy Knapp said. "Chad grew up along the coast."

"You stupid bastards!" I kicked back hitting shins and threw elbows to break free of Sarge's arms, then raced upstairs. "What goes to sea during a storm washes ashore."

All but forgotten was my aching face. I had to get outside and find Chad. He was out in the storm all alone, but if there was any way to hang on, he would.

I raced down the hallway toward the room we had shared. Kenny Mashburn had gotten our attention by hammering on the door. Chad wasn't doing that. It meant he was unconscious and could wash up anywhere. Wash up against anything, and anything could wash in over him. The thought of the breakers that jutted into the ocean made me shiver. I had to hurry.

In my room I snatched up my fanny pack and strapped it on. That done, I pulled on my rain gear and my baseball cap, then ripped the sheets off the bed, and as I passed the closet in the rear of the house, brought along several of their kin. Down the hall I saw the men staring at me. Perry Jackson and Jeremy Knapp had reached the top of the staircase.

I ignored them and went up the stairs to the third floor—where horizontal-rolling shutters covered the windows. I found a window overlooking the side of the house above the porch. I wasn't a complete idiot. I wasn't going to take on the storm headfirst, nor did I want to reach the ground. The ground, for all intent and purpose, would no longer be there.

The rooms on the third floor were smaller and had fewer furnishings. As I worked the flashlight around, I saw the room held a straight-backed chair, a floor lamp, and a trunk. The chair and lamp were both covered in plastic.

Downstairs I heard Sarge calling to me. Some foolishness about what in the hell did I think I was doing?

You jerk, I'm going to save my fiancé like you should've done. You and all your training from your hitch in Operation Desert Storm. In the rear. I locked the door of the room, went to the attic window, and threw it open.

Horizontal rolling shutters have a top and bottom track attached to the house on the outside, and, when closed, they are fastened together by a clip. The tracks for the shutters extend horizontally beyond the window, so when you push or pull the shutter, they either open or close. The shutter runs along the track.

I removed the clip holding the shutters together, ran the shutters back, and got a mouthful of rain. The wind forced me back, and I had to hold onto the sides of the window to stick my head out and look below.

I could make out the porch roof and that is where I

had to go. Everywhere appeared to be under water, and the only light spots were from the froth of the storm. The ocean was coming ashore, and with each wave, much higher each time.

Not being a qualified web slinger, I tied the sheets together to form a rope. I figured to reach the roof and swing down to the porch. There was still a chance Chad was on the porch, a chance that Sarge and Jeremy had lied to keep from opening the door.

Or to get rid of Chad. And think it would get rid of me. Well, maybe it would. Maybe it had.

Behind me, Sarge pounded on the door. "Miss Chase, don't go out there!"

"Susan, are you nuts?" screamed Jeremy, with the funny sound he made talking through his nose.

There was more pounding on the door, and by the time I had hitched myself over the sill, serious discussion was being given to knocking down the door. That, courtesy of the shrill voice of one Reynolds Pearce.

"She's got a window open in there!" he screamed. "Break down the door. We have to close it."

But I was gone, having tied all the sheets together and grounding them to the straight-backed chair.

Because of how I'd tied the sheets, the chair straddled the open window. Sliding down the sheet, I heard the door giving way. Probably Perry Jackson and one of his boots.

Then I was on top of the metal roof of the porch. Very quickly, and holding onto the sheet with one hand, I rolled over the side to take a look. Thankfully there was no gutter, and I was able to shine the light on the porch.

The wind picked at me and tried to pitch me off. It was going to be dicey getting down, and the porch was underwater. I must've looked like a spastic Spiderman as I slid, first my feet and then my legs, over the edge of the roof.

Then, just when I had my torso over the edge, the sheet was suddenly jerked up, and I found myself being scraped across the roof. Literally scraped, because the roof had some very sharp edges.

"No!" I screamed. I would not be pulled back into the house!

With rain in my face when I looked up, I tried to see the window. It was there and no one in the opening.

Check that. Perry Jackson now stuck his head out, and sheltering his eyes from the rain, he stared down at me and shouted.

That's why I'd been short-sheeted.

The men had pulled the chair away from the window so Sarge could stick his head out and plead with me to return to the house.

Hell, I didn't think I had the strength to climb back up, much less hold on forever with the wind pushing me back and forth across the metal roof. I had to get off this roof. I was beginning to pick up more than one cut or abrasion.

Sarge continued to shout at me, but nothing could be heard over the wind. Rain pelted me, the wind tore at me, and the world was very dark. I tried to remember what time of day it was but couldn't.

Probably not important. Daylight or dark, I had to get down to the porch and use my light to find Chad.

Once again I loosened my grip on the sheet and slid forward on the wet, metal roof of the porch. From there, I peered over the side. As I said, luckily there were no gutters, so I could lean over and point my light at the porch. More plastic garbage cans, lawn furniture, and the occasional piece of plywood meant for someone's window floated past.

No sign of Chad.

It goes without saying I was fairly hysterical by then. What brought a shock of consciousness and reality to me was when Sgt. Perry Jackson joined me on the roof. And Sarge didn't use the sheet to lower himself to the rooftop.

He landed in a "splat" beside me. The action so startled me, I loosened my hold on the sheet. That didn't make any difference. The sheet was loose and so was I.

I reached out and grabbed Perry. Before he could slide over the roof and fall into the shallows, I was able to use him as a handhold and swing over the railing and drop onto the wraparound porch.

Sarge landed in the waves and was sucked away, then just as quickly washed toward the porch. I stuffed the flashlight into my pocket, zipped it up, and grabbed one of his arms, my other gripping the railing. The receding surge was pulling Perry away from me.

I shouted his name.

He didn't hear me or couldn't.

Then he was gone, jerked away and pulled out to sea. I gripped the railing to maintain my footing in the water on the porch and stared into the gray of the storm.

Where I looked there was no berm, no shoreline, no breakers, only dark water reaching around all sides of the house. On hands and knees, and with one hand always on the railing, I kept the bill of my cap down and floundered around the side of the house to escape the wind.

The surge found me and sucked me back. Luckily I rammed into the railing, if you want to call it luck. I hit hard and felt a sharp pain in my side.

Perry Jackson was back. When I fought my way to the porch steps I found him tangled in the railing, so I was able to get a hand on him. From the corner of my eye, I could see the ocean lapping at the edge of the front doors, with more water being thrown in curtains, not sheets.

The porch was practically underwater, and I could barely find a handhold. Where was Chad?

Into the wind, I screamed, "Chad!"

I admit I got pretty crazy for a while, but it was a very short while. The ocean swept across the deck, and Sarge, with no pulse, washed down the side, taking me with him. We were pulled under as the surge fought to gain mastery. Hell, give the storm it's due. It mastered us.

We were washed around on the wraparound porch with my feet and one hand reaching for something to stop my motion, and generally being slapped by either the side of the house or the balusters of the railing. I was kept busy protecting my head from a good thumping.

Water sprayed in my eyes. I barely had hold of the hand of the dead man, and every time I opened my mouth, I got more saltwater in it. Finally, I realized I wasn't doing Chad any good by continuing to hold onto a dead man. I let go of Jackson and gripped the railing with both hands as the ocean washed across it.

It didn't take long for Sarge to disappear. When the surge receded and headed out to sea for another run at the house, Sarge went with it, and this time he stayed. Perry Jackson had come to this house to exact revenge on those he believed had driven his sister mad. Now he, too, was gone.

That, however, was no longer my business, if it ever had been. I pulled out my light and worked it around the porch.

Empty.

Then I checked the water washing around the house.

Nothing but a few timbers from someone's pier.

Gripping the railing and stumbling around to the far end of the wraparound porch to the shell parking lot, I held on tight and used my light to watch a fleet of six or seven foam pillows sailing across the parking area.

But no Chad.

"Chad!" I screamed again, and the wind tried to fill my mouth with both saltwater and rain.

I remained there for a few minutes, working the light around but saw nothing more than debris being washed ashore. I slogged through ankle-deep water to the other side of the house. There I worked my light around in the dark of the tides that coursed between the house and the palms on the far side. I saw nothing more than a metal shed, submerged and bobbing in the surge.

Down the beach, palms shimmied in the darkness, clouds appeared close enough to touch, and the world remained a melancholy gray. Whatever wasn't lashed down moved when the waves hit it. Though I've lived on the water all my life and have taken to many a sea, this was weather I could not comprehend. Where was a witch when we needed her?

"Chad!"

Give it up, said a voice inside my head.

"Chad!" I cried even louder.

Get back in the house before you drown.

I've lasted this long . . . .

Get back inside before you end up with more than cracked ribs and abrasions. Chad is gone!

No! Don't say that.

The voice was even firmer now.

Get back in the house before you're washed out to sea.

A decent argument was made when the water on the porch rose to my waist for several moments. I burst into tears as I turned and headed for the door. Maybe someone would be fool enough to open it one more time.

Yeah. Right.

The wind screamed at me and doused me with rain, but from inside the house there was only silence. As I pounded on the door, there was no clamoring to let Susan Chase inside. I'd been abandoned to the elements.

When I turned around to lean against the shuttered double front doors, I saw the shed floating in my direction, a black blur in the gray darkness. Through the cotton stuffing my head, it finally dawned on me that the shed was going to smack into the house right where I stood.

Turning, I slipped and fell to my hands and knees as the ocean pulled me toward it. The shed smashed into the railing, broke through, hit me, and everything went very dark.

Chapter 15

I was floating on my back. I tried to orient myself
but could see nothing. The clouds shut out the daylight, if there was any, and the rain spanked my
face—probably what I had to thank for waking me.

Turning my head hurt. I tried to figure out where I
was. With the movement of the tide, I finally realized I
was being pulled out to sea. That got me moving.

I fought with the ocean to return to the land. What
land, I didn't know, but I wanted to be on any sort of
ground.

The ocean couldn't have cared less. It drew me down
into its depths, and I had only a brief chance to grab a
rain-filled breath before it sucked me under.

It was dark underwater, even harder to understand
that water pressure only causes the sea level to rise
more than one or two feet. The wind was my enemy, and
that wind drives waves commonly called the surge. As
we move toward land, I found a landmark and realized
it was a palm—still anchored to the ground.

Looking around, I tried to locate my next point
of reference—like what I would smash into. A tall
structure loomed in the darkness.

We, meaning me and the tidal surge, or waves, were headed in that direction. I gulped, taking in some saltwater, and wanted to scream in frustration as the power of the storm forced me forward, horizontal to the ground.

Oh, God, this was the way it was going to end. I was going to be plastered against that structure, feet first, then swept out to sea. Just like what had happened to Chad.

What had happened to Chad?

I wasn't supposed to die. Neither was Chad. The wedding was all planned. Chad would exit the Rainey Sculpture Pavilion ahead of me at Brookgreen Gardens, and when the all-girl rock and roll band played the Wedding March, Harry Poinsett would escort me from the Pavilion restaurant, where we would walk toward the center of the park. To Diana's pool—Diana of the Chase, that is. Harry wouldn't have it any other way.

Harry Poinsett is a member of the Huntington Society, or folks who donate thousands of dollars to Brookgreen Gardens. Those contributors can have weddings performed in the park. Yes, yes, I know you're not supposed to take wedding photographs on the property, but if my friend Jacqueline and her James Bond camera are on the job, there will be plenty of prints for all.

Now none of that will happen. Instead there would be a memorial service for Chad and me. But no bodies.

I sailed forward, unable to stop my movement as the surge took me inland. The structure was a house and I was headed for its roof. It was a tall sucker, and the closer I came I realized it was the knockoff Victorian mansion.

Oh, God. That's all I needed. To be killed by that damn house.

As I was swept forward, the surge lifted me until I could finally take a breath. Still, the house didn't move. I was on a collision course, and then suddenly the surge and I were sailing across the porch.

I missed a post by inches, its roof by the same amount, tweaking my toes with enough pain to make me realize I was still alive, and when the surge returned to sea, I fought it. I didn't want to go back out there.

The storm didn't care. It tugged me back to sea, and when the surge faltered, I was unceremoniously dumped on the porch again, hitting my head.

Cripes, but that hurt!

Still, I remembered to throw out my hand for a handhold as I was pulled down the same steps where Chad had disappeared. I was coughing and crying, screaming, and grabbing for anything.

That would be the bottom of the railing, which was unfortunately under water. I held my breath as the surge receded, then it was hand over hand and crawling toward a porch almost under water. Grasping the railing, I hauled myself to my feet so I could finally breathe.

I blinked back tears and watched as the waves backed off and gathered strength for another run. My eyes burned from the saltwater and my hair clung to my face. I raised a weary arm to wipe the moisture away, then gripped the railing.

The same surge that had killed my boyfriend and ruined my life was headed in my direction. I removed my Smith & Wesson from my fanny pack and took dead aim at the surge approaching the porch. As the storm rushed ashore, I slowly squeezed off one shot after another, right into the gut of the storm.

The surge, or waves about ten feet high, was fifty feet away and my hammer was clicking on empty when I heard someone inside the anteroom shout, "Stop the shooting! Hear me? Stop!"

The surge was less than forty feet away when my hands dropped to my sides and I stared at the door. My ankles were covered with water.

"That you, babe?"

"It's . . . me."

The door was unlocked, the shutters covering the front doors opened, and Kenny Mashburn emerged, no worse for the wear. The surge was less than thirty feet away as a foot of water washed through his ankles and into the house.

He saw the pistol. "Hey, babe, you can put that gun to better use inside."

I didn't understand what he was saying. I stood there, mute and stunned with wonder that the door was open.

The surge continued its race toward the house.

"Look, babe, you coming in or not. If not, I just might join you outside." Kenny saw the surge . . . less than twenty feet away. "Then again, maybe not."

Kenny grabbed my arm and began to pull me into the anteroom. The surge was ten feet away when Kenny finally dragged me inside.

Then the water was in the narrow room, washing us into the house. Water rushed down the hallway and toward the rear of the house. Kenny bounced off one wall, then across the hall to the other. I was sucked under, where something in the back of my mind told me that this was not a good idea. I floundered to the surface after slamming into the wall and feeling the indenture of a picture frame square against my back.

Kenny washed past me. He appeared unconscious. I grabbed the jamb of one of the pocket doors, and with my free hand slapped his dark face. He came alive, dark eyes staring at me, looking around and taking in the totally new environment.

"We've got to get upstairs or we're going to drown."

He looked toward the door, a murky piece of light down the hall. "What happened?" He touched the back of his head.

"Some dumb-ass opened the front door and saved my life."

A crooked grin crossed his face as I held him on the surface. "Babe, I always was the man for you."

"And full of it, too." I kissed him on the cheek.

"Hey, babe, that's sweet, but it's not safe in this house. I seen dead people."

"And I lost a fiancé."

The words hit me and I burst into tears. My sobbing was uncontrollable. Chad was gone! Gone forever. Our life together was gone! My heart ached, my face, arms, legs, too, but my chest was empty. Everything I'd worked for in the last few years had been swept away by this son of a bitch hurricane. I could hear the grandfather clock bonging madly, signaling the passing of my future.

Kenny was holding me by the shoulders, shaking me. "Babe, you okay?"

I hardly heard him. All I was thinking was could I rebuild my life? How many times had I put my life back together? After my brother and sister had died, and Mama had walked out on us, and Daddy had gone over the side of the shrimp boat . . . the barrel of a pistol was looking really good. All I had to do was suck on—

"Babe, you're making me nervous. Talk to me. This ain't like you."

The wind and rain taunted me as the storm continued to roar, unrelenting, unrepentant. The surge was retreating from the house, sucking furniture with it.

The Queen Anne chairs in the living room were the first to go. The storm had taken Chad through that same set of matching doors and there was nothing I could do about it.

Why'd I let him talk me into coming here? Why hadn't I refused to come?

Because I had to protect him.

But I hadn't. I'd lost him to this damn storm.

Kenny was being pulled in the direction of the open door as the surge retreated from the house. The table that had subbed for an altar followed him. When it almost hit me, that got me moving.

"Kenny, grab hold of something!" I let go of my handhold and went after him.

He got his hands on a picture fixed into the wall in a manner where it could not move.

It moved, ripping off the wall and sending Kenny pinwheeling toward the front door.

I met him there, holding onto the jamb of the pocket door that led to the living room. Gripping the edge of the jamb with my fingers, I got an arm around him and jerked him into the living room.

Turned out to be just in time. Riding the retreating surge, the bonging grandfather clock smashed into the doors as Kenny and I were sent spinning into the living room—where we crashed into the window. The glass held but the curtains did not. They, however, were not hooked to the cornice, and that's what we held onto. I blinked in astonishment as the camp stove floated into the grandfather clock, bounced off, and careered around the corner. Kenny grabbed it and held on tight.

He was too heavy and both he and the stove went under. Again I fished him out of the drink and dragged him over to the cornice, the only dry spot remaining on the ground floor.

I looked across the hallway. "Kenny, we've got to get upstairs." Crossing the hallway would be like crossing a swollen creek.

"You got any more ammo for that piece?" he asked.

"What? What does it matter?"

"If you ain't got more ammo, we're in deep trouble."

"What are you saying?" We needed to reach higher ground, not spend our last minutes drowning.

"Unless you figure ole Kenny had good reason to toss that big white dude out that third-story window, there's two other guys in here and they'll be waiting for us when we try to go up them stairs."

Chapter 16

"**K**enny, what are you talking about?"

"I've seen one hell of a lot of dead people while I've been in this crib, and I gotta tell you, babe, I think the brothers and the 'hood ain't so bad, no matter what the eleven o'clock news says."

"What dead people?" Was it possible that this fool had recovered Chad body?

"I'm just minding my own business—"

"Kenny, cut the crap. Give it to me straight, or when I get my strength back, I'm going to dunk you until all your air bubbles out."

"Now, babe, that's no way to treat someone—"

"I feel the strength returning to my arms. Tell me what happened to Perry Jackson and make it quick." Seeing dead people—I don't think so.

Watching the furniture being lifted and washed out of the living room and into the hall, the sleazeball said, "All I knows is that I sees you runs upstairs and these three white dudes go after you. I'm thinking I got no business in what's going on, but I figure since it was probably you that makes them white boys open the door and let me in." He smiled a crooked smile. "Or that you're so handy with that pistol they just had to. So I kinda trailed along. Say, who was that white boy got washed down the steps? He really your fiancé?"

I nodded, and then looked in the direction of the kitchen where the water washed into the back corridor. "I had my wedding gown picked out. It had spaghetti straps, a spray of Venitian lace appliqués encrusted with pearls in a flower shape in a descending pattern. It was a floor-length sheathed gown that reached my shoes and the train was removable. For dancing. I was going to dance the night away with Chad."

It made me want to cry. J.D. Warden, Mickey DeShields, and my new boss, Theresa Hardy, had all chipped in or I never could've afforded such a dress. Actually, on counters and desks up and down the Grand Strand, more than one cop had placed a ten or twenty in a mayonnaise jar labeled "Get Susan Chase off the street."

"You didn't need to come to this house, Kenny."

The dope dealer glanced toward the next floor as the sea water washed around us. The water was cool and murky. Seaweed clung to my legs, or I hoped that's what it was.

"You got that right, babe. I seen too many dead people in this house."

"You're beginning to repeat yourself."

"Like I said, when those white boys started upstairs after you, I figured I better go along and see if you needed my help."

"What bull! You knew I had the pistol, the one I used to make them open the door."

One hand came up in surrender, the other clung to the cornice. "Okay, okay, I was just trying to play catch up."

"Go on."

"They'd gone through another door and up to the third floor. When I got there they were hollering for you to come back inside and you had to hurry because they had to close the window. 'Shutter it' I think was what they said. There were some kind of an argument between a blond guy and a guy with Kleenex stuck in his nose and this really big guy in army clothes."

"What were they saying?"

"Arguing over what to do with you."

"What did they think their options were?"

"Haul you back inside or untie the sheet."

"Which one wanted to untie the sheet?"

"The large one they called 'Sarge.' He said you were a danger to the house. That they had to button it up. Look, babe, I think—"

"I don't want to hear what you think. I want to know how the one called 'Sarge' landed on the roof."

Kenny nodded as a chair from the study floated by. Soon it was headed for the logjam of furniture at the single open front door. Outside the door the world remained gray, and the only light we had was from my flash, stuck in my breast pocket and pointing straight up. To a ceiling coming closer and closer. We were going to have to move to higher ground, but first I wanted to know what I was up against.

"The blond guy and the guy with the paper sticking out his nose convinced Sarge to give it one last try."

"Such a small window," I said, shaking my head. "He must've been leaning way out when he fell."

"Fell, babe? That dude was pushed."

"By who." I'm sure the shock registered on my face.

"By both of them."

"Jeremy and Reynolds?"

"I don'ts know any names. This Sarge guy didn't want to help you, but the guy with the Kleenex in his nose said the big guy was the only one with the authority to make you do anything. The blond-headed man was nodding like crazy and saying Sarge had to give you one last chance."

"Go on."

"I tell you, babe, that Sarge dude didn't want any of that action, but he handed off the chair to the other two and stuck his head out the window and shouted at you again. The big dude's shoulders were sticking out of the window when the two other dudes looked at each other, dropped the sheet, and shoved him out."

"Jeremy and Reynolds did this."

"If that's their names."

"Then what?"

"Hey, babe, I worked the streets long enough to know when I seen something I don'ts need to remember. I gots outta there."

"And went where?"

"Well, I thinks I got it made when you opens that front door and I'm out of the storm, then five minutes later I'm seeing all these dead people."

"Kenny, you did not see dead people. You saw someone murdered. There's a difference."

He shook his head. "I slid down them stairs to the second floor and ran into the hall. I shoulda kept going, maybe back into the storm. I ran into this small room at the back of the house. Across from the john."

That would've been the room where Chad had held me when I'd broken down and cried, and it gave me no satisfaction I had been right that I didn't belong here. Neither had Chad.

"So you opened the closet and found a dead girl."

"Yeah." He looked at me. "You know about that?"

"The blond-headed man stashed her in there."

"He stash the one in the bathroom, too? Lots of blood on that white girl and she was in the tub. I was thinking I could hide behind the shower curtain, but all that blood got to me."

"How long did this take?"

"About a New York minute. It don'ts take long for me to put distance between me and dead people. That's when I heard the shooting and knew you were trying to catch ole Kenny's attention from outside." He watched a bag of potato chips float by. "Hey, lunch is served." He snatched up the bag.

"Not yet." I took the bag away and stuffed it above the cornice. Ten-foot ceilings and eight of those feet gone each time the surge came through the front door. "I want to see what we can do to close that door."

Kenny peered around the corner to the hallway. A procession of chairs from the dining room bobbed and floated, heading for the logjam at the door.

"I don'ts see anything we can do about that, babe. We've got to get outta this water. It's getting chilly, and if you not gonna let me have those chips, I need to check out the kitchen. It's gonna be under water soon."

To underscore his point, the soup pot floated in our direction. The pot had been cleaned but not put away. Now it washed toward the door as the storm continued to fight with the entrance, trying to pry open that other front door.

Under our feet we could feel the suck of the ocean as it came and went. I swam in the direction of the front door and had plenty of help. The storm was intent on pulling everything out of the house, and with one door open, it had a decent start. Kenny used one piece of ballast after another to cross the hall.

"Er—babe?" Kenny was floundering behind me. "There's something I gots to tell you."

"You don't know how to swim."

"Yeah."

"And you've lived at the beach all your life."

"Actually, I come down from Newark five or six years ago. I hate them winters up north."

"How lucky for the Grand Strand."

"Hey, I'm just trying to make a living. I ain't hitting folks over the head and making them take drugs."

"No. Junkies hit people over the head, steal their money, and then buy drugs from you and every other dealer along the Grand Strand."

"What people do with their lives ain't necessarily my problem."

To this I said nothing.

There was quite a traffic jam at the front door. The sofa had gone first, and been thrashed around, back and forth, until it busted out the other exterior door. The Queen Anne chairs and the table bumped into the walls, then the doors, backed off and took another run at the main entrance. During all this, the grandfather clock continued its muffled bong as it sank below the surface of the water.

"This isn't going to work." There was no moving any of this stuff—by me or by Arnold Schwarzenegger.

"What we gonna do?"

"Let me think."

Jeremy didn't give me the chance. From a landing, he shouted, "Hey, who opened the door?"

"Kenny let me in."

"You were stupid to go out there in the first place," yelled Reynolds, and then followed Jeremy Knapp past the first turn in the stairwell.

"Why'd you do that, dumbass?" asked Jeremy.

"Where you get off calling me names?" hollered Kenny. "We're all in this together."

"We wouldn't be," said Reynolds, "if you hadn't opened the door."

"Chase was outside."

"And soon you will be." Jeremy no longer wore the tissue stuck up his nose and his voice had returned to normal. He disappeared above us, finishing the last turn in the winding staircase.

I pushed a dining room chair out of the way and swam over to the stairs, where I gripped the railing. Kenny struggled along behind me, using the furniture to keep his head above water.

"We're coming up."

"The hell you are," said Reynolds, moving upstairs and giving his partner-in-crime a hand with whatever Jeremy was doing. "I just got rid of one killer. I don't want another one up here."

"You're admitting you killed Perry Jackson?" I looked for Jeremy. "From what I hear, you had some help."

Reynolds glanced at Jeremy, who was wrestling with something out of my line of sight on the second floor. "It was either him or us, Susan."

"It was self-defense, Chase," called Jeremy.

I grabbed the railing and hauled myself up the stairs to the first landing. Behind me came a very loud thump as I reached back to give Kenny a hand. When I turned around to go up that part of the staircase mounted along the wall, I saw a dresser had been moved to the next landing. Now Jeremy and Reynolds gave it a shove.

On its back, the dresser slid down the stairs toward me. I stumbled into Kenny, who was right behind me on the landing, and pushed him out of the way more with my elbows than my hands. We landed on our hands and knees in water to our waists.

Kenny saw the dresser and looked up the stairs to

where Jeremy and Reynolds stood on the next landing.
"What you do that for?"

"We don't want you up here."

"Because I'm going to send both of you to prison."

"If you survive the hurricane," shouted Reynolds.
"And hypothermia." He disappeared from sight.

"I've got a weather radio," Jeremy added. "It says the
eye of the storm is over Wilmington right now."

That was par for the course. Wilmington was a
magnet for every storm that came ashore along the
Carolina coast. Outside, the wind sounded like a train
passing through, and the water level approached the
first floor's ceiling level.

"And don't think about coming up the back stairs.
Reynolds is taking care of that right now."

We heard something crashing down the back stairs
where it splashed into the water.

Jeremy said, "You stay in your part of the house and
we'll stay in ours."

"So you've decided to kill us? Where will that leave
you when all these bodies begin to wash up along the
Grand Strand?"

"I'm disappearing, too, Chase," said Jeremy, glancing
toward the rear of the house. "I've got more than one
passport and I don't fancy doing time."

"For assaulting a SLED agent or for poisoning Helen
McCuen?"

Another piece of furniture tumbled down the back
stairs, one we did not hear splatter in the water. That
could only mean it had become lodged in the stairwell,
blocking access to the second floor.

"Chase, I didn't kill anyone. It was all Perry Jackson.
He set this whole deal up."

"And sent out the invitations? Where did he get
everyone's address?"

"Helen did that for him. All Perry had to do was show and start killing us. And he did." Now Jeremy smiled. "Or rather, he tried."

Reynolds appeared, red-faced, to stand next to Jeremy at the first landing. "You won't be using the back stairs. I've got them blocked."

"What you trying to kill me for?" demanded Kenny as he leaned into the railing on the lower landing. "What'd I ever do to you?"

"Collateral damage," said Jeremy without any feeling in his voice.

He looked at me. "What's that mean?"

"You just happened to get in the way."

"He didn't just happen by," said Jeremy, heading up the final flight of steps. "He came to a hurricane party. Just like you, Susan."

"Yeah," said Reynolds, following Jeremy to the second floor, "we're not responsible for either of you."

"You white people are crazy!"

I tried to reason with one of them. "If you killed in self-defense, Reynolds, you won't let us die down here."

Reynolds, however, had disappeared on the second floor, so I moved to where the dresser lay on the staircase, jammed into the floor of the first landing.

"Susan," said Reynolds over the scraping sound of something being dragged across the upstairs hallway, "I've survived one killer and I don't want another up here."

"So I'm a killer now," I said as I climbed over the dresser that lay on its side on the stairs clinging to the side of the interior wall.

"That colored boy with you. He's a dope dealer. Everyone knows him."

"You got that right, white boy. You and your buddies

gots my cell phone on speed dial."

Reynolds saw what I was doing. "Susan, don't come up here."

Jeremy appeared at the top of the stairs with another dresser. Very quickly I crawled over the dresser jammed into the first landing, but when my wet feet connected with the slippery stairs on the other side of the dresser, I went to my hands and knees.

As I scrambled toward the next landing, the dresser came hurtling down. I jumped back as the second dresser hit the wall, careered off it, and headed in my direction.

Over the railing I went, landing in the water with a splash, then a groan as I hit something submerged. Slowly I swam over to the first landing, where Kenny waited.

"Look out, babe!"

I did a jackknife and forced myself under. A lamp made a circular impression on my shoulder as I touched bottom. I swam to the hallway where Jeremy and Reynolds couldn't see me, burst to the surface, and brushed hair out of my face.

"You okay, babe?" asked Kenny from the landing.

"Thanks . . . thanks for the warning."

As we watched, the dresser that had come sliding at me was stood upright. That was followed by a chair crashing into the upright dresser against the one lying on its back across our path upstairs. Reynolds and Jeremy were building a wall between us and the second floor.

"And there's more where that came from," said Jeremy, his voice disappearing as if he was headed to find another dresser to send our way.

I didn't doubt it. Once they had the dressers where they wanted, pieces of bedding would follow. After that, all they had to do was wait for the tidal surge to force us to the base of the staircase, where it would be like shooting fish in a barrel. If we didn't die of hypothermia.

My teeth chattered, but no one could hear them over the sound of the wind. The surge returned and tried to wash me down the hallway. Grabbing the wall, I held on so I wouldn't be washed into the rear of the house.

A lamp came sailing in the direction of Kenny, and he threw himself into the water.

He came up floundering and splashing around, looking for something to grab hold of. The surge caught him and washed him down the hallway. I swam to him and told him to turn over so I could get an arm around his chin.

"Look, Reynolds," said Jeremy from where furniture was piled on the staircase. "Chase has become a lifeguard again."

Another lamp soared down and hit Kenny in the leg.

"Man! That hurt!"

Jeremy laughed. "Looks like your part of the house is taking on some water."

In the relative safety of the hallway, I turned Kenny over and pushed him against the jamb of the study door. He reached down and touched his leg.

"Anything broken?" I gasped.

All this treading water was getting to me. If I did somehow reach the second floor, I wasn't going to be in much shape to take on two men who probably worked out. And, as Kenny had pointed out, there were no bullets in my gun.

Oh, well, who comes to a hurricane party with an extra clip? The pistol was to keep the predators away after the storm, not give me the upper hand when it came to homicidal maniacs.

Kenny said something about his leg, but I wasn't listening. I had to think. Still, Kenny babbled on.

"Shut up, Kenny, and let me think."

"Babe, I'm starting to gets cold."

"That's the wind through the door."

"Your teeth are chattering, too."

"I'm just scared," I said with a smile.

"Susan Chase scared? That'll be the day."

Kenny glanced at the logjam of furniture being washed back and forth in what remained of the anteroom. The last of the interior doors was rocking, set free by repeated blows from the surge. When it went, the furniture and anything not tied down would wash out the front door.

Including us.

Kenny shivered. "Are we gonna have to go outside?"

Shaking my head, I said, "I don't want to be in that storm again. All sorts of stuff's floating around."

"What other choice we got? Those two honkies won't let us upstairs."

"I wouldn't either. They're both going to prison."

"Yeah. Right. On whose testimony?"

"Yours."

"Babe, I 'preciate the thought, but I can't swim, and you can't keep your head above water much longer." He glanced toward the spiral staircase. "Those white boys have fixed my black ass for good."

"Not if I have anything to say about it."

"Chase," he said with a laugh, "you always had more balls than brains. What's the plan?"

Chapter 17

Only by retreating to the kitchen could I get a chance to think, away from the storm and the taunts of Jeremy and Reynolds.

Okay, okay, maybe they'd stopped taunting me, but I was really feeling rotten about what had happened to Chad. I had to get away and have a good cry. That wouldn't inspire much confidence, so I positioned Kenny where he could hang on to the cornice, safely away from the storm surge.

Once I'd finished my cry, I dried my face with one of the rolls of paper towels remaining on the top shelf, and that gave me an idea.

Outside, the storm continued its assault against the house. Still, the water on the first floor appeared to have stabilized at about six feet, with surges to eight. That's when it became dicey. The ceilings were only ten feet.

The double doors that closed off the rear of the house from the front waved back and forth with the surge, and the dining room door was jammed shut. During an earlier reconnaissance, I had learned that the dining room table could not be sucked through the door and it had jammed the door shut. At the time, I didn't know that was good news.

Kenny was happy to see me return to my place in the water at the cornice, then stared hard at me. "What's wrong, babe?"

I touched the side of my head. It might be a concussion, cracked ribs for sure, and a fractured arm. Along with numerous cuts and bruises that stung in the saltwater. "Jeremy hit me before you arrived."

"I mean your eyes. They're puffy."

"Saltwater doesn't agree with me. That's why I went to work for SLED."

Kenny loosened his grip on the cornice, grabbed the jamb of the pocket door, and peered around the corner. There was nothing but an opening where the two sets of former doors had been, and all the first floor furnishings were gone, plus those pieces thrown down from the second floor. The ocean had literally sucked everything out of the house.

He returned to the cornice. "I hope you got a plan. I don'ts know how much longer I can hold on."

To the stairs, I shouted, "Jeremy! Reynolds!"

"There's just me. Jeremy went to use the john. Aren't you glad he didn't stick his butt over the side of the railing and use your water."

"I doubt the plumbing works."

"Don't worry about us. You're the one with problems."

"I want to talk to Jeremy."

We had to wait until he returned.

"Chase, you still with us?"

"Jeremy, I want you and Reynolds to allow Kenny and me to come upstairs. We're not going to last in this water. If hypothermia doesn't get us, the storm will."

Someone tossed Chad's pack over the railing. "Maybe there's something in there you can use."

Kenny lunged for the pack, but I pulled him back. A footstool followed the pack into the water.

"That's attempted assault," I shouted.

Both men laughed, and Jeremy said, "Yeah, but who's going to be around to press charges."

"I'm giving you one last chance. I want Kenny and me to be allowed to come upstairs. Do you understand?"

"Go screw yourself, Chase."

"You assholes," shouted Kenny. "I'll cut your balls off if you don't let me up there."

"Us," I whispered.

Mashburn glanced at me. "Oh, yeah. Us!" he shouted to the stairwell.

Jeremy's voice trailed off as if he was heading for his room. "Just go away and die."

"I have instructions for you, Jeremy. Reynolds, you'd better make sure Jeremy knows what he's to do."

"What I'm to do?" Jeremy laughed, returning to the railing. "Why in the world would I listen to you?"

"Because there are knives in this kitchen—"

"And we've already shown you what's going to happen if you try to come up these stairs."

"Jeremy, come to your senses. If you had nothing to do with the death of Helen McCuen, then what you are doing is cold-blooded murder."

"Chase, you begin to bore me."

"Reynolds," I shouted, "you want to go to prison? Possibly risk the chair? I can talk to people, speak on your behalf, but if you insist on doing things the hard way, you'll suffer the consequences."

More laughter from upstairs and something said by Jeremy to Reynolds about not wanting to be bothered again unless we tried to come upstairs.

"When we come upstairs you're to move to the third floor. I will lock you there until the National Guard arrives in a couple of days. If there's any food, it'll be provided from—"

"Shut up, Chase."

"As long as both of you know what you're to do when Kenny, who's an expert with a knife, reaches the second floor."

"Susan, you aren't going to reach the second floor."

"Reynolds, promise you'll make Jeremy move to the third floor when Kenny and I come up. We don't want to have to kill anyone."

"Bold talk for a drowning woman," Jeremy said. "Teeth chattering yet?"

In fact they were, as were Kenny's. Still, that would all end soon.

"I just want you to know what I, an agent of the State Law Enforcement Division, expect of you. I'm depending on you, Reynolds, to make sure there is no more resistance." I glanced at Kenny. "I don't want to have to turn Mashburn loose on you."

Kenny's eyes were wide. "Babe," he said in a hoarse whisper, "I ain't no knife fighter."

"They don't know that. To them you're just another dude with an attitude." I pointed upstairs. "You going to let those two white boys keep you down?"

"Son of a gun," he said with a grin, "and I thought I was a silver-tongued devil. You and me, babe, we'd get it on"—he gestured at a room that had been cleansed of everything but the cornice we hung to—"if it wasn't for the hurricane."

"Sure, Kenny, the death of my fiancé and the storm can't dampen my spirits for you jumping my bones."

"Susan," said Reynolds from upstairs, "I've told Jeremy as you asked me."

"Does he understand?"

"I understand that no girl's coming up these stairs and neither is your friend." This from Jeremy.

I smiled at Kenny. "Ready to do this thing?"

"You damn right." He tried to high-five me and fell into the water.

I pulled him out. "Save the celebrating for later. Right now, we need to build a fire under these boys."

Kenny watched as Chad's pack was sucked out of the house and disappeared into the darkness. "That oughta be a trick in all this water."

Kenny and I retreated to the kitchen where we dove for treasure, actually knives. We found the largest and the handiest, and when Kenny surfaced, he scrambed onto the island built into the floor. Joining him, I plunged one knife into the ceiling—below the floor of the room Chad and I had once shared.

"We gonna dig a hole through the ceiling?" Kenny was openly skeptical.

"No," I said, holding up the rolling pin. "But I do need a hole." I loosened one of the handles of the rolling pin and handed it to him. "Think you can put several holes in the ceiling around the kitchen without getting the one over the island wet?"

Kenny glanced at the water swirling around his waist. "I don't know, babe."

"You get this particular hole wet and we're going to be down here an awfully long time."

He set his jaw. "Then I'll do it."

"Give me a minute," I said. "You need a distraction. And remember, there are things to stand on everywhere: counters, tabletops, and appliances. You don't have to tread water."

I let the water pull me out of the kitchen. Keeping my feet in front of me, I was able to maneuver into the short hallway, past the back staircase where furniture was jammed so we couldn't reach the second floor. I negotiated my way through the double back doors that washed back and forth with the surge, then floated toward the front staircase.

When I tried to climb the winding staircase, a table lamp was thrown at me. I dove into the water and returned to the cornice in the living room.

I slammed my hand on the wall. "You bastards are going to let us die down here." I slammed my hand against the wall again for emphasis.

"Hey, if you can't run with the big dogs," said Jeremy, "stay on the porch."

I slammed the wall again. "This isn't right," I shouted as I hit the wall with my fist, and careful to use the arm I did not think was fractured.

Through the front door, the wind moaned like Marley's ghost. Still, that was not enough noise to cover up Kenny's destruction of the sheetrock ceiling in the kitchen so I continued to complain and slam my hand against the wall until Reynolds said, "You brought this on yourself, Susan. You didn't have to come."

"You bastards . . . ." I slammed the wall a few more times for good measure. "When I get up there—"

"But you're not going to get up here," said Jeremy indifferently.

I let them think I was crying, hysterical, hitting the wall again and again. Then I returned to the kitchen, where Kenny had the makings of more than one hole. Evidently he had dog paddled over to the stove, the sink, and the tabletop and put holes in the sheetrock over each one.

Nodding my appreciation, I didn't stop him but swam into the pantry and reappeared with several rolls of toilet paper held high overhead. Gasping, I joined him on the island.

"That gonna take forever unrolling toilet paper, and we're gonna get some of it wet."

"Just put the rolls inside this hole. I have an accelerant."

He placed one roll in the hole over the island as I plunged back into the water and swam into the pantry to retrieve several rolls of paper towels. When we were through, sweat ran down Kenny's face and he had to use a paper towel to wipe it away.

"You got matches?" The obvious question.

I took off my fanny pack and took out a tube. I passed the stubby cylinder to him. "Don't open it yet."

I swam over to the potato chips. The lantern was gone, as was the camp stove, all victims of the surge, but I had stashed unopened packages of chips on the shelves over the fridge, thinking we'd need something to eat that wouldn't become waterlogged. It hadn't been lost on me that when I had returned from my good cry that the chips I'd stashed in the cornice beside Kenny were gone, and I didn't think they'd been washed away by the tide.

Taking two sacks of potato chips, I returned to the island. After catching my breath, I shook off any water, opened the first bag, and shoved it into the hole between the sheetrock ceiling and the plywood sub-flooring above it. I moved rolls of toilet paper onto the open bags and the scattered chips.

"It's gonna smolder more than burn," complained Kenny.

I grinned. "That's just fine with me."

"Oh," he said, joining my smile, "you was serious, girl. You gonna smoke them out for sure."

"Well, they are a couple of insects, aren't they?"

"You got that right."

I had to deter him from giving me a high five and dousing our escape plan.

In the light from my flashlight stuck upright in my jacket pocket, I took the small metal cylinder from Kenny, dried it with a paper towel, and then opened it and took out a match. These tubes come with a rough portion on the surface, and I stuck the cylinder in the hole overhead and struck the head of the first match.

When the match lit, I touched off the potato chips. The chips flared up, began to burn, and then began to nip at the ends of the toilet paper and paper towels. I did another bag of chips like the second, and then Kenny and I were forced out of the kitchen because of the smoke and the stink. Burning chips give off a god-awful smell.

Floundering into the hallway and trying to keep Kenny's head above water, I was about to sink myself. Still, I was able to get out, "We've got to close some doors."

"In this water?"

Kenny stared down the hall at the open front of the house. All four doors appeared to have been ripped off their hinges, but we couldn't be sure. There was only the light from a lantern from the second floor illuminating the staircase; after that our world ended in darkness.

"The ones we need to close are these." I pointed to the double back doors separating the front of the house from the rear. "Otherwise the wind might suck the smoke out the front of the house."

He looked up the backstairs jammed with furniture, including a mattress on top of two matching dressers. His face broke into a wide grin. "There's no door upstairs and no way for those guys to get away from the smoke."

I returned his grin. "Unless you move to the third floor."

Seeing a wisp of smoke float out of the kitchen and above the surge level, he asked, "How we gonna do it?"

I held up the skeleton key. "The way the doors move back and forth, we use the surge when the doors move the proper way and then lock them and hope for the best."

We waited for the surge to help us, and finally got both doors shut. Now all we had to do was wait on the potato chips, toilet paper, and paper towels. Trapped in a narrow space, they would smolder and burn. Some of the tissue would actually burn, but most of the paper would send out lots of smoke into a very small area.

First the section between the ceiling and the water in the kitchen and pantry would fill, then the dining room, with its large table jammed against the door. Prompted by air through other holes knocked in the ceiling, which would feed the fire from different directions, the smoke would ultimately find its way upstairs. But the fire needed time to smolder.

"Kenny, you need to return to the cornice."

The drug dealer stared at the grayness outside the house, the wind and rain blowing through, and the waves lashing the interior.

Over chattering teeth, he said, "With—without you?"

I nodded. "The cornice is the same place it was and I need a distraction."

"So they don'ts know about the fire."

Again I nodded. Or was that my teeth chattering? "Nothing says Jeremy can't wet the floor of the room above the fire. I doubt they will, but they might open the window and let the storm in to put the fire out."

"Not those dudes. This storm scares them."

"Same as it does you and me." I shoved him across the hallway and into the former ritual room. "Now, go tell those two white boys what a real wuss I am."

"What you gonna be doing?"

"I'm going to check on the fire."

It was better than I expected. I only needed to swim to the door of the kitchen, where I found the area between the surface of the water to the ceiling thick with black smoke. Gasping for breath, I surfaced near the double doors, which I had to pry open to get a little air.

Once I regained my strength, I slipped through, locking them behind me, and floated to a point where I could hear Kenny telling the guys he had plenty of nickel and dime bags and that's why he'd come to the party, that could he buy his way onto the second floor.

I let out a shriek when I heard this.

More laughter from the second floor.

We were dealing with some really sick puppies. Oh, well, power corrupts and absolute power sucks you down to your emotional bottom.

Kenny pleaded with Jeremy and Reynolds and they continued to laugh. Then, in an act of heroic stature, Kenny let go of the cornice and allowed the storm to suck him into the hallway.

"Kenny!" I shouted.

But he wasn't a complete dummy. He had waited until the surge entered the house, so he was able to cross the hall and reach the stairs. There he caught a baluster and hung on.

Grinning, he turned to me as he pulled himself up the stairs. "Hey, they can kill off Kenny on 'South Park,' but not me!"

"You idiot," I shouted as he started up.

Those upstairs answered with a hail of drawers, lamps, and pictures thrown like Frisbees. They all bounced off Kenny. Mashburn had found a plastic garbage lid and was using it as a shield to reach the first landing. He started up the stairs that climbed the interior wall.

Jeremy and Reynolds shouted warnings to each other as my knight in shining armor struggled over the dresser lying on its back. He pulled himself up the railing with one hand, the other shielding him from whatever they could throw in his direction.

It didn't take long for those at the top of the stairs to bring out the heavy artillery. A chair was thrown. It barely missed Kenny as he struggled over a dresser. There he regained his footing at the final landing, only five steps from the second floor. Out came a knife as he started toward them, garbage can lid in one hand, butcher knife in the other.

"Now, boys," he shouted, a maniacal grin on his face, "prepare to meet your maker."

I had followed him to the first landing on stairs awash with water. Getting to my feet, I saw Jeremy and Reynolds holding a mattress upright at the top of the stairs.

"No way, black boy." Reynolds laughed. "This is definitely above your station."

The two of them stepped forward with the mattress and pushed Kenny back. The knife and the garbage can lid were no match for the thickness of the mattress. They forced Kenny back to the upper landing, then down the stairs and over the dressers. He lost his balance and tumbled back to the lower landing, which was under water.

By then, I had slipped over the railing, grabbed the balusters, and begun to swing up the side of the stairwell mounted on the interior wall of the house. As I climbed toward the second landing, hand over hand, the plastic lid and butcher knife went flying and Kenny fell back and splashed to a stop on the first landing.

"Hey, boy," shouted Reynolds from the landing, "don't forget who's king of *this* hill."

Another lamp was thrown, but Kenny dodged it as he dove into the water. Now Jeremy and Reynolds were free to turn their attention to me. I had made my way hand over hand to the second landing, despite the pain in my shoulder and an ache running up a forearm. If I could only make it to the second floor . . . .

Jeremy bent down and looked me in the eye through the balusters. "I never did like you, Chase."

And before he could kick my fingers, I dropped back into the water and dove for Kenny.

Chapter 18

Two days later the National Guard moved in and sorted out the sick, the lame, and the just down right stupid. I had no ID as it had been lost in the storm, so I was shackled with the others and led off to a detention center. Finding so many dead bodies in one house had made the National Guardsmen slightly nervous.

My new boss was there to interrogate me. "You tried to burn down a house?" asked Theresa Hardy.

"It seemed like the thing to do."

I lay across an arm, facedown on the interrogation table, exhausted, arms shackled. The National Guard had fed us, but I had not caught up on my sleep. In addition, I had a nasty cold and couldn't shake a bad case of the jitters. At the slightest sound, I would jump and my shackles would rattle.

"There are so many bodies . . . I can't believe . . . ." This included the body of one Perry Jackson, which, ironically, had been washed back into the house unknown to any of us on the second or third floors.

I looked up from the table. "Sometimes that happens when you attend a hurricane party."

"And that's enough in itself to have you scheduled to visit our shrink again."

"Whatever," I said with a loose gesture of my hand and rattling my handcuffs.

I put my face against the cool of the gray interrogation table and shifted around the shiny, metal shackles that held my hands and feet. There was also an orange jumpsuit, but the black spot was on my heart.

"Susan, we need to talk further."

At least that's what she later said she told me. However, I was asleep, and I slept for two days straight. When I woke, the bad news began. They had found Chad. There would be no wedding.

I rolled over, sobbed into my pillow, and refused to talk with anyone. A series of people trooped through my hospital room. First Theresa Hardy, who tried to intimidate me, then J.D. Warden, who tried to reason with me, and finally Mickey DeShields, who actually cared. I said nothing, and when they were at their wits' end, Harry Poinsett came by to tell me that he had returned *Daddy's Girl* to its berth next to his at Wacca Wache Landing.

"It survived the storm?" I asked, eagerly.

"Yes, Princess, and so did you."

"But Chad . . . ."

Harry surveyed the stark and brightly lit hospital room. There was no one in the adjoining bed. A handcuff linked me to my bed.

"I will take you to see him." Harry stopped. "When you're ready."

Evidently I wasn't ready. I rolled over, faced the wall, and wept.

They left me alone for seventy-two hours straight. In the fog of my condition, I remember J.D. Warden saying to the doctor, "Chase always wants to give you a piece of her mind. Isolate her until she's ready to talk."

I didn't think that was quite fair, but at that point I really didn't give a damn.

When supper was late the third day, I started banging on the wall. They had not answered my repeated punching of the call button.

Finally, a nurse appeared.

"Am I going to get something to eat or what?"

"I'll check on that." She was the night nurse, a tall, gangly woman.

A half-hour later, Harry Poinsett appeared at the door. In his hands were a recorder and a chili dog from Sam's Corner. I greedily gobbled down the chili dog and gulped the sweet tea. There was even ice cream. My favorite. Rocky Road.

Harry placed the recorder on the bed and turned it on. "Two dead girls were found on the second floor of the house."

I explained how Reynolds Pearce had stashed Vicki and Helen in an attempt to make everyone think there was someone else in the house.

"I thought all of you stayed together," said Harry, gesturing with his hand. "You know, to make sure the killer wasn't left alone with one of you."

I shook a head that contained a headache the size of Texas. "When Reynolds was sent to watch Jeremy's door, he grabbed Vicki and stashed her in the bathroom. That took only seconds."

"But there was no blood on Pearce's clothing."

"There was plenty of sheet to wrap her in."

"And you believe he had the time to snatch Helen McCuen from the living room and take her upstairs?"

"Sure. Chad . . . and Jeremy were fighting in the hall. There was plenty of time, and distractions."

"This investment banker from Charlotte planned all this mayhem and murder?"

I shook my head.

When I wasn't more forthcoming, he added, "There were two young men on the third floor. The two Kenny Mashburn said shoved Perry Jackson out a third-story window. The National Guard had the devil of a time talking Knapp and Pearce into opening the door. Both kept jabbering about a crazy black man with plenty of knives. Both Knapp and Pearce were dehydrated and incoherent. What water they had, they'd used to dampen their shirts and stuff them against the bottom of the door so smoke couldn't seep through."

"They didn't have anything to worry about. I went back downstairs and put out the fire once we controlled the second floor."

"Susan, I have to tell you that was a damned dangerous thing to do. How did you handle the smoke trapped between the ceiling of the first floor and the rising water level? It couldn't have given you much room to maneuver."

"I had a baggie. From my pack on the second floor. I simply took the air and my flashlight with me."

Harry shook his head. "You make it sound so easy."

I smiled. "Being inside a burning building during a hurricane gives one the proper motivation."

"Then Jeremy Knapp masterminded this mass murder?"

Because my head ached, I didn't shake it. "No, Dads. Perry Jackson thrust the screwdriver in Helen's chest. He didn't know she was practically dead from all the arsenic Jeremy had been feeding her the last few months."

"And all this happened because of a competition between Jeremy Knapp and Helen McCuen?"

"All this happened because Helen McCuen wanted to strut her stuff. By gathering those who had participated in the Waties Island affair, she could force them to realize, if she hadn't already, that, she was going to leave them in her dust by establishing a worldwide coven of witches."

"But she didn't actually think—"

"That she could turn back the storm?" I struggled up against my pillow, and the tape recorder started to slide off the side of the bed. I snatched it before Harry could, and smiling through the pain rocking my head, chest, and arm, I placed it on the bed next to me.

"Lili was the most erratic storm to hit the United States since the 1900s. Witchcraft or not, Helen had a fifty-fifty chance of turning away the storm."

"So Perry Jackson, or the one you called 'Sarge,' killed the others?"

"If you mean Vicki Hester and Brandon Calhoun, yes. I became the wrinkle in his plan. But he would've killed me, too. Once Perry Jackson arrived at that house, no one was going to leave alive."

"But when you were interrogating everyone, you sent Sarge to your room. Evidently he wasn't a suspect or you wouldn't have done that. Your Smith & Wesson was in your fanny pack. Which begs the question: Why didn't Sarge simply shoot everyone?"

"Stab wounds with jagged edges, like a screwdriver, are more convincing when bodies wash ashore. Think of all the creatures that can feed in those holes."

A look appeared on Harry's face as if he didn't actually want to understand this particular point.

I moved on. "Sarge couldn't steal my gun, Dads. It would've cinched he'd come to the house to kill everyone. Besides," I said with a careless gesture of my hand, "I'm fairly sure Perry had a weapon of his own in the bottom of his duffle bag. He was, after all, in security work."

"But Helen McCuen solicited assistance from his security firm."

"And if someone were to dig deep enough, I think they might find a salesman at Jackson's firm who was encouraged by Perry to contact Lady Light. Witches are subject to all sorts of harassment, and that's why many become solitary practitioners or gather in covens in the woods. Not because there's something inherently wicked about witchcraft, it's a benign sort of paganism, more like tree huggers, but the harassment—"

"By normal folks," suggested Harry.

"If you want to call the rest of us normal. Anyway, Helen's desire to show off, not the norm for your average wiccan I might point out, played into the hands of Perry Jackson, though I doubt she knew who he was. But Sarge knew her. He'd gathered dossiers on everyone in the house."

"Except you."

"That would be true," I said through tearing eyes.

Harry leaned back in his chair. "The way you describe Helen, she would be just the sort of weirdo to request Perry Jackson—if she learned the girl left on Waties Island was Perry's sister."

"That possibility exists."

He shook his head. "The people you hang around, Princess, even consorting with drug dealers."

"Kenny Mashburn put his life on the line for me."

"But I can't understand why you don't blame him for what happened to Chad."

I turned away and faced the wall. I knew what had happened to Chad, and it was enough to cause my shakes to return. Once I regained control of my breathing, and my nerves, I could face Harry again, but only after wiping away more tears.

"Chad lived along this coast all his life, spent hours

on the ocean, some even in storms, but he couldn't comprehend the power of a hurricane."

"Or live with himself if he didn't do the right thing by allowing Kenny Mashburn to come in out of the storm?"

"Well, Dads, that's not a problem he has to deal with any longer, is it?"

Chapter 19

Skylyn Institution is for assisted living, and it's where I would see Chad the first time since the storm. As I entered the automatic front doors, I was surprised to find J.D. Warden sitting in one of the white rocking chairs on the front porch.

No longer with SLED but retired, Warden spends most of his time fishing along the Grand Strand. Northies are like that. It's not a bit like fishing in the East River for corpses. I shivered, and it had nothing to do with the AC.

"What are you doing here?" I asked, wincing. My ribs hurt now that I had gone cold turkey off the medication.

"Came to see the Rivers boy."

Hair black and slicked back like basketball coach Pat Riley, and wearing another of his off-the-rack business suits, Warden appeared to be dressed for success, not retirement.

"Sure that's the reason you're here?" I asked.

"I'm not here to baby-sit you, if that's what you're thinking, Chase."

"Like it would have to be done," I said, entering

the lobby, where more people were grouped in wheelchairs.

"You've always needed someone to point you to True North," said Warden, trailing me.

I shook my head but stopped, as that hurt. Something to do with a separated shoulder that was connected to the neck bone that was connected to the arm bone that was fractured. One arm worn in a sling. There was also a slight limp, if you're keeping score for the bad guys. Or the hurricane.

"Chase, what would you be without people like me?"

I turned around slowly, stopping the ex-cop in his tracks. If I was going to dress up and play the part of a grownup I wasn't going to take this. I might even hit him with my purse. "I don't need anyone."

"And that's what you're here to prove today."

"You son of a bitch."

I stalked off. Still he followed me. I had no clue what his game was.

"You've been fractious ever since you tried to save your girlfriends from those white slavers. It really hurt when one of them regretted not staying with her master, didn't it? Sort of shook your independence to the core."

I said nothing. I had someone to see. Someone certainly much more important than this jerk.

Warden continued cracking on me, and me, I couldn't hobble fast enough. "You just don't get it, do you? Not everyone's tough enough to face the next day, followed by the next. But that's what has to be done."

I stopped, turned around, and planted my feet. "Just what the hell are you doing here?"

He smiled. "I'm here to see a friend of a friend."

"You don't have any friends," I said, turning away once again.

"And you?"

"I have plenty."

"Most of them are dead, and you still have to go on."

I felt my cheeks and neck flush. What did this man know about growing up on the street? Taking care of yourself. Always being on the lookout. And always looking for a way out.

"That's why it was so important to rebuild your life with the Rivers boy, wasn't it?" asked Warden, as if reading my mind.

"He's not a boy."

"I've heard you refer to him, and other young men, as 'boys.' I never understood why you would use that term, but it's appropriate."

"Tell me about it, you armchair shrink."

"You're still looking for your daddy, but he's gone like the rest of your family."

"Get away from me, you bastard," I threw over my shoulder.

"I'll get away from you when you start making some sense."

I stopped again and faced him. "Why do I get the feeling you're trying to make me?"

"Because that's all men have ever wanted. They want to conquer you—Susan Chase, the ultimate challenge."

Tears filled my eyes and I returned to limping down the hall. "Chad never did."

"And where is he today?"

I whirled around and slapped him. I slapped him more than once. Surprisingly, he stood there and took it until someone gripped my arm. Harry Poinsett.

I let Harry take me into his arms. Tears ran down my cheeks, and not only from the pain in my shoulder, arm, head, and ribs. The good news was that J.D. Warden had disappeared. Good that he had. I might've killed the sumbitch if he'd stuck around. Of course, there was the little matter of the aching head, arm, and ribs.

"There, there, Princess," said Harry, stroking the back of my head, my short blond hair, and barely touching the sling. Dads always seems to know what I need. He's not the jerk J.D. Warden has always been.

"I don't know what to do, Harry. I feel . . . so lost."

"Things have not turned out as you wished. Lieutenant Warden had his way of helping. I don't know what'll work. Any way you do it will be tough." He leaned me back where I could see him, then glanced at a door down the hall. "There is no medicine like hope, no incentive so great, and no tonic so powerful as expectation of something tomorrow."

Tears ran down my cheeks. "Dads, some days I don't think I can go on."

"We can all go on. It's whether it's done with style that matters."

I laughed and cried, all at the same time.

"You're Susan Chase," Harry said with his charming smile. "Would you know anyone with more style?"

Susan Chase had style? More likely she groped her way along. "Faking it until we make it" we call it.

"You can do this," Harry said.

I looked at the door down the hall and shuddered. A real old person inched along on a walker. That guy had nothing on me. My heart felt as old as the Sphinx, and just as dry. "You think so?"

"You've lost others and gone on."

"I . . ." My head dropped. "I never lost anyone like . . . Chad."

He held me tightly. "You can do this, Princess. That's what J.D. Warden was trying—"

Jerking away, I said, "He didn't do such a good job!" More tears as the pain hit me again. I wiped them away. Lucky the girl who doesn't use much makeup. Yeah. Real lucky.

"Susan," said Harry, gesturing toward a door at the end of the hall. "Do the best you can do."

I nodded—at what, I don't know. I had no clue as to how I was going to handle this. Chad's mother had briefed me, but that wasn't anything you could take to the bank. Lois Rivers would lie for the hell of it.

Taking a breath, I faced the door, then stepped over and gripped the knob. There had been many a door I had gone through, sometimes wearing a bulletproof vest. This time it was just me, and there was no bad guy on the other side. Simply the man I loved. Still, when I opened that door, he would not be home.

Turning away, I let go of the knob and faced Harry. "I can't do this."

"You need a sense of closure. You must do this."

Tears started down my cheeks again. I hastily brushed them away. My legs shook. Literally. Nodding a trembling chin—my face must look like a puffy mess—I faced the door, then opened it and walked into my future.

Chad sat with his mother on a sofa against the wall. Straight ahead of me was the hospital bed, but there were no IVs or other hospital paraphernalia; just a bed turned down if the patient felt tired and wanted to rest. Both Chad and his mother smiled as I stood there, gripping the door, holding onto it for dear life.

"Look who's here, darling," said Lois, letting go of Chad's hand. "It's Susan. Come here, dear, and have a seat."

Two matching chairs stood opposite the overstuffed

sofa, and I stumbled over and held onto the back of one of them. Something solid felt very good in my hands.

Chad was dressed in a yellow pullover shirt and tan slacks. On his feet were a pair of socks and slippers. His tan had disappeared, his hair was down across his forehead, and I felt the same old urge to brush that unruly mop of brown hair back.

But I couldn't. He might take that as a threat. Or an invasion of privacy.

"Hello," said Chad with an innocent smile. It was distinctly not that special smile meant for me.

I had to sit down. Before I fell down. I did, facing the two of them.

"Susan came to see you today, dear." Lois brushed back the unruly hair across my former fiancé's head.

I gritted my teeth.

Chad smiled and stared at me.

I said hello.

He said hello.

I said it was nice to see him.

He said it was nice to meet me.

And I lost it.

I found myself in the hall being comforted by Harry. It was a moment before I could control my tears. I was sobbing to the point that a nurse made her presence known.

"Does she need something, Mr. Poinsett?"

"No, no," said Dads, allowing me to lay my head on his shoulder and sob like crazy. "She'll be fine."

Glancing at the doorway, the nurse said, "Did she know Mr. Rivers . . . before?"

I felt Harry nod.

"Then it must be quite a shock. Amazing. To come out of a storm like that with only a bump on the head."

Yes, lady, but one hell of a bump. He didn't remember anyone, especially me.

I started crying and clutching Dads. The nurse put a hand on my shoulder and patted it. Lois opened the door and said the noise was upsetting her son. Shaking out of Harry's grasp, I walked away.

Harry tried to follow, but I waved him off. "I need a moment."

I entered the ladies room.

No one there.

And me not in my main man's head. He didn't remember his mom, his dad, his boats, or me. Only his mother was allowed to see him. Chad didn't know her so there was no way he could handle a relationship.

With me.

Gripping the edge of the wash basin, I stared into the mirror. Eyes red, hair a mess, and a look on my face I'd seen more than once before. Little Girl Lost.

My shoulders slumped. I was all alone once again.

Well, never let it be said of Susan Chase that she wasn't a woman of action.

I fumbled with my purse, jerked out my Smith & Wesson, and took a breath. I flicked the cylinder and checked the load. All full but the chamber where the hammer rested. Taking a breath, I looked at myself in the mirror, said good-bye to Susan Chase, her sorry-ass past, and her empty future.

I couldn't do it.

The sight of me with a gun at my head was almost comical. Still, I didn't laugh. I turned away from the mirror and faced the stall as the thumping of feet in the hallway ended at a door opening behind me.

Got to do this quickly if I'm going to do it at all.

I raised the gun to my temple, fitted my finger inside the trigger guard, and—

My hand was knocked away. The pistol discharged and the bullet slammed into the Formica wall, bounced into one of the stalls, and ricocheted around until it came to rest, rolling from under the stall's wall.

A skinny black girl fumbled out of a door. A lit cigarette hit the floor as she scrambled past me and J.D. Warden. A pack of cigarettes followed the butt to the floor.

"Keep them! I ain't never smoking another." She raced out the door.

Harry Poinsett came through the door. He stared at me as tears ran down my cheeks and my shoulders slumped. In Warden's hand was the Smith & Wesson.

"Susan, did you really . . . ." Evidently, he couldn't finish the thought.

Warden opened the chamber and emptied the rounds into his hands. "Women slit their wrists, never mussing their hair. But not this one. This one always thinks she can do anything like a man."

I whirled around, and ignoring the pain, began to pummel him with my fists. "You . . . ."

Warden slapped away my hands, then slapped me.

It rocked me and I stumbled back, falling into the wall and gripping the hand dryer to stand.

"Why'd you stop me?" Tears continued to run down my face, and it wasn't just from his slap.

"I'm not finished with you yet, Chase."

"I think I'd better take her home," Harry said.

Warden stepped between us. "She doesn't need you. She needs me."

✳　　✳　　✳

It was a hot day and my back ached and my arms were sore and smoke was in my face. We were clearing the road entering Francis Marion National Forest; you know, like the guy in the movie, *Patriot,* about the Revolutionary War.

J.D. Warden worked beside me, and for an old guy he did pretty well. Of course, he did tend to hog all the drinking water. I stood up and wiped the sweat away. My tee hung on me, soaked, and stares from men working with us had not been lost on me.

"Means you're on the road to recovery," Warden had said earlier in the day.

"You know, I'm getting a little sick and tired of working alongside Kevin Costner."

Warden gestured at the burning timbers next to the road. Warden's blue tee hung on him and he hadn't shaved. His stubble was gray. His face tan, and he seemed quite pleased with himself.

"Susan Chase with an attitude is good?" I asked, with a laugh. "J.D., you have come a long way."

Warden tossed another branch into the fire. The orange and red flames stood out against the green of the swamp. We were burning so the dry spell after Hurricane Lili didn't cause a forest fire. Smokey the Bear were we, men and women assisting the forest service.

"Chase, I've slept on that houseboat of yours for more than a week. Do you think tonight you might let me get a good night's sleep?"

"Oh, you finally getting tired of tying me into my bunk every night?"

"That and the sound of a woman calling for someone who no longer exists."

My face heated more than from any fire and I glared at him.

Very quickly, my keeper added, "I'm not as young as I used to be."

"I don't think you were ever young, J.D."

I wiped more sweat away by raising my healed arm and felt a breeze on my tummy. Several yards down the road, someone dropped their end of a log. Another man screamed.

I smiled, and Warden saw it.

"I think I'm done here," he said.

Warden picked up the pack, the one he had borrowed from me. After emptying the water bottle and slinging the pack over his shoulder, he said, "See you around, Chase."

"Not if I'm lucky."

A small smile was all I got for my crack.

"Will you be returning the pack?" I inquired.

Warden shook his head as he walked away. "Won't be returning at all. A buddy from NYPD said 9/11 was enough for him. He retired to Whitefish, Montana." Warden stopped and glanced past me in the direction of the ocean. "Out there, I hear, the country is totally unlike Myrtle Beach. The women, too."

The anniversary of 9/11 had come and gone, so I felt compelled to ask, "And when did you receive this invite?"

"About a month ago."

"Before the storm?" I was plainly astonished.

Warden raised a dirty hand and pointed a finger at me. "Don't go there, Chase, or you'll inflate your value out of all proportion to what it really is in people's lives."

Sanctuary of Evil
A Susan Chase Mystery

It appeared that Myrtle Beach PD was looking for someone to talk down a jumper.

"Can you take this one?" asked Dispatch.

"Don't you have someone else?"

"I was told to route everything to you."

"Every dirty little job that comes along," I muttered.

"What was that?" asked the voice over the radio.

"The Host of Kings Hotel, you say?"

"You got it." And the radio in the sedan went silent.

My partner sat in the passenger seat. Daphne Adkins was a bony woman with long arms and legs.

"We're catching a jumper?" she asked.

I said nothing, only wheeled the sedan around and headed in the direction of the Host of Kings.

My partner peered at me through the uneven darkness of the Grand Strand. "Have I done something to tick you off, Susan?"

I smiled at her. "Just your being here ticks me off."

I guess I should introduce myself.

My name is Susan Chase, and these days I'm an

agent of SLED, South Carolina's equivalent of the FBI. My family used to fish the Florida Keys, and Daddy pursued that career up the East Coast until reaching the Grand Strand, always one step ahead of the bill collectors. After Mom walked out on us, that left Daddy and me, fussing and fighting until one night, drunk, he fell overboard and drowned.

Being only fifteen, my next stop was a foster home, where it took me only a few weeks to gauge my chances of becoming the next Cinderella. I hit the streets and lived by my wits, taking a job guarding the beach, and during the off-season, waiting tables. Then some guy asked me to find his kid who'd run away from home. From there I became a private investigator, then an investigator for SLED. Which brings me to the trainee who accompanied me the night I took the call that practically ended my career with SLED.

A crowd had gathered in front of the hotel. Just what a jumper wants. Someone to beg him not to leap to his miserable death. If that's what this guy expected, Dispatch had picked the wrong gal.

Climbing out of the sedan, my partner paused to stare at the idiot illuminated at the edge of the roof of the hotel. After all, this is Myrtle Beach, and there's little that isn't highly illuminated once the sun goes down. I shook my head and headed inside where a uniformed patrolman stopped me.

"Sorry, Miss, but . . . ."

His voice trailed off as he saw the SLED ID on the lanyard around my neck. I pushed my way past him and toward the bank of elevators, where another cop checked my ID before my partner and I were allowed upstairs. Noticing one of the hotel staff near reception, I motioned the guy over as I pulled off my long coat and the business jacket that was part of my navy blue pantsuit.

"Let me have your jacket."

"My jacket?" asked the blond guy, whose name tag said "Eric."

"And give me a woman's name tag and outfit my partner the same way."

Moments later, we took the elevator to where a couple of cops and a firefighter huddled in the stairwell.

"What you doing here, Chase?" Earl Tackett was a stocky guy with a buzz cut and pecs that came from working out. He had twenty years in the military and was working on another twenty with the Myrtle Beach Police Department.

"I'm your negotiator."

"That's bull," said his partner, another well-built guy in the same blue uniform and equipment belt. "This is more of your grandstanding, Chase."

Tackett glanced at the firefighter and reached for his radio. "I'll have to check this out."

"And while you do, hope the guy doesn't go over the edge."

"Hey, we've got someone watching him," said Tackett's partner.

"But is he near enough to prevent the idiot from going over the side?"

"Nobody can get that close."

"That must be why Dispatch called me."

"Listen, you guys," said the firefighter. "They said a negotiator was coming up. If it's Chase, it's Chase. Let's get on with it."

After pocketing my lanyard ID and switching my weapon and extra clip behind my back, I handed off my long coat and suit jacket and shrugged into the hotel's maroon one. I'd already transferred my pad and pen. To the guys, I said, "I want this door secured and I don't want your people on the roof."

Tackett nodded, then cracked the door and ordered another cop into the stairwell. Daphne and I took the patrolman's place as the door clicked shut behind us.

The roof's blacktop was covered with pebbles, and here and there were huge air conditioners and stubby pipes. It wouldn't normally be all that chilly up here, but a wicked breeze had kicked in from offshore.

"Don't come any closer," said the figure at the edge of the roof.

"I'm with the hotel, not the cops." Lowering my voice, I said to Daphne, "Stay at the door." At this point I was about forty feet away from the guy. "My boss told me to get the info. That's why I'm here." I opened the jacket with both hands as I walked his way. "They sent a girl to talk with you so you wouldn't be afraid." Now I was about thirty feet away.

The guy was middle-aged, balding, and had a beak for a nose. His face was red from the sun and especially that beak. He wore a pair of plaid shorts and a beach shirt from Ripley's, the aquarium, not the freak show.

"I need to know your room number." Out came my pad and pen from under my jacket.

"Room number? I don't have a room."

I stopped twenty feet away. "Look, fellow, this is not a smart move—to leap to your death from our hotel roof."

"Why not?"

"Our lawyers will have a field day."

"Lawyers? What lawyers?"

"The suits who'll contest any settlement." I turned to Daphne and told her to tell the cops and firemen they could vamoose.

"What was that all about?" asked the guy, stepping away from the edge.

"Mister, you're going to make more profit for this hotel in one minute than it'll make all month."

"How's that?"

"We'll collect on your insurance money."

"But my wife's the beneficiary."

"Sorry, but the hotel has an army of lawyers who will contest the payout."

"But my—my family will need the money."

From next-door someone yelled "jump!"

The dummy nodded in agreement. "That's right . . . I have to jump."

"Well, before you do, think about it. If you were staying here, your family might have some wiggle room—a guest wandering about in an area left unsecured, but . . ." I shrugged. Up and down the Grand Strand green and red lights danced. It was near Christmas and once again I had no one to celebrate with.

"You're trying to trick me. They'd have to pay."

"Mister," I said, stopping less than ten feet away, "the last guy did this, the home office collected a half a million bucks. I hear the guy's kids are working their way through college."

"I—I don't understand. Why are you telling me this?"

"I had to work my way through school. Work and study, work and study, that's all you have time for." I glanced at my trainee who stood at the door to the stairwell. Lowering my voice I said, "You're lucky Daphne's not clocked in yet. She'd push you over the side to earn another promotion."

The man gaped at the bony woman near the door.

I shivered in the breeze off the ocean. I was missing my long coat. "Look, Mister, can we get on with this?"

"You want me to jump?"

"No, but it's damn chilly up here."

"But if I was a guest . . . ?"

I smiled. "Now you've got it."

"And I can jump anytime, right?"

"Sure," I added, continuing to smile.

"Okay," he said, crossing the pebble-strewn blacktop. "Let's go downstairs."

After he passed me, I said, "Er—mister, it really doesn't work that way."

Before he could respond, an explosion rocked the Grand Strand. Looking toward the center of the Strip, I saw the night light up over the Pavilion and all the rides.

About the Author

One of South Carolina's most versatile writers,
Steve Brown is the author of *The Charleston Ripper*,
a novel of suspense set in modern-day Charleston;
The Belles of Charleston, a historical novel set in
1856; and *Carolina Girls*, a portrait of what it was
like to vacation on the Carolina beaches in the
sixties and the seventies. You can reach Steve at
www.chicksprings.com.

If you would like to read more about Susan Chase,
please ask for her books by title and number:

Color Her Dead	ISBN 0-9670273-1-4
Stripped To Kill	ISBN 0-9670273-3-0
Dead Kids Tell No Tales	ISBN 0-9670273-4-9
When Dead Is Not Enough	ISBN 0-9670273-7-3
Hurricane Party	ISBN 0-9712521-5-7
Sanctuary of Evil	ISBN 0-9712521-6-5
The Charleston Ripper	ISBN 0-9712521-0-6

CPSIA information can be obtained
at www.ICGtesting.com
Printed in the USA
FFOW04n0834181114
8822FF

9 780971 252158